HIGH VALLEY MANHUNT

All Laramie Davis wants is a hot meal. What he gets is a plate full of trouble. It starts with the killing of a deputy sheriff in Rock Springs and goes downhill from there. Laramie tangles with outlaws, blood-hungry Indians and a murderous posse led by a family of killers. Before it's over, many men will die . . .

B. S. DUNN

HIGH VALLEY MANHUNT

Complete and Unabridged

LINFORD
Leicester

First published in Great Britain in 2015

First Linford Edition
published 2018

A catalogue record for this book is available
from the British Library.

ISBN 978–1–4448–3725–4

Published by
F. A. Thorpe (Publishing)
Anstey, Leicestershire

Set by Words & Graphics Ltd.
Anstey, Leicestershire
Printed and bound in Great Britain by
T. J. International Ltd., Padstow, Cornwall

This book is printed on acid-free paper

This one is for Jacob, who always asks, 'And then what happened?'

1

'What do you think, Bo?' Laramie Davis asked his big Appaloosa Stud. 'Does it look like a good place to get a nice, hot meal?'

The board said Rock Springs. Population 942 but by the look of the sign and its crossed-out numbers, it was obvious that the population was on the decline. Nestled at the foot of a snow-capped mountain range that towered overhead, the town was surrounded by low ridges, topped with Ponderosa Pine and Douglas Fir, that ran the length of the spacious valley. Laramie cast his gaze over the vast tracts of grazing land dissected by cottonwood-lined creeks, with clear waters, fed by the slow ice melt from above.

Bo stood silently, and flicked his dark tail at an annoying fly. The big horse's front half was a chocolate colour that became dappled on his hind quarters.

'Yeah,' said Laramie in answer for his horse. 'Let's go find out.'

As the afternoon sun sank lower in the cloudless sky, Laramie urged Bo forward with pressure from his left knee. In response, the animal started forward, on the deeply rutted trail as it wound down the slope, and ran them straight into trouble.

★ ★ ★

Inquisitive townsfolk stopped to stare at the stranger who rode his fine chocolate coloured Appaloosa along main street. The man, they guessed was maybe forty-five, of solid build and a touch over six feet tall. He had brown hair to match his eyes and his face was tanned and weathered, witness to the long trails he'd ridden over the years. He wore dark jeans, a red shirt and a dark vest under a buckskin coat. His saddle boot held a Winchester rifle, 1876 model, but what drew their attention, were the twin Remington six-shooters holstered on his slim waist. The weapons indicated to all around him, that the stranger was a gunfighter.

As he proceeded down the street, he rocked easily with the smooth gait of the appaloosa, aware of the attention he attracted. Experience had taught him that strangers in some towns had problems, especially in his profession. Gunmen attracted trouble like a moth to a flame.

The town, like many others Laramie passed through, had false shop fronts which lined the dusty street. There was a bank, post office, stage and freight company, dry goods store and a few cafes. A hotel sat between the cattleman's association building and the Red Eye Saloon. With a slight nudge, Bo changed direction and walked up to the timber hitch rail outside the bustling saloon.

Laramie swung down out of the saddle and looped the reins over the rail. He stretched then slapped the built-up trail dust from his clothes.

From habit, he adjusted his gun belt and flipped the rawhide loops off the hammer of the Remingtons. No such thing as too careful he thought, with death only a bullet away. His right hand on the polished walnut butt of one Remington, Laramie climbed the scarred wooden steps and eased his way into the saloon.

The bar room covered a large, well-lit area that included a section set up with a roulette wheel and felt-covered poker tables.

The afternoon crowd was of a reasonable size and the noise was at a medium level. Voices grew louder as liquor consumption increased. Raucous laughter cut across the room, followed by the shrill screech of a whore's indignity. Laramie looked left and right as he moved further in. The sound of breaking glass was quickly followed by a savage curse. Wooden chair legs scraped the timber floor as two men lurched to their feet, only to be restrained by friends. Faced with a possible threat,

Laramie had half drawn the Remington, but now eased it back into its well-oiled holster.

He sidled up to a long, Mahogany bar with a brass foot rail and polished counter top. The red headed barkeep was busy with a ranch hand when he saw Laramie and gave him a nod.

'I'll be with you in a minute,' he called above the din.

Laramie lifted a hand in acknowledgement. He watched the barman finish with his customer then make his way along the bar towards him. 'What can I get you stranger?' he asked, jovially.

'Beer,' said Laramie.

The barkeep smiled warmly. 'Sure, beer comin' up,' and he walked off, found a mug, filled it and brought the large, foam covered beer back to place it in front of the gunfighter. Laramie tossed a dollar onto the counter top but the barkeep pushed it back. 'First one is on the house.'

Laramie nodded. 'Obliged.'

Laramie looked around the room then asked, 'Do you serve meals in here?'

'Sure do,' the barkeep answered. 'What would you like?'

'What have you got?'

'How about I get the cook to run you out a rump steak with all the trimmin's. You can follow that up with a piece of pie.'

Laramie's stomach growled at the prospect. 'Sounds great. I have a horse outside at the rail that needs takin' care of before I eat.'

The barman nodded that he understood. 'Sure, sure. I'll have your meal waitin' when you return. The livery is just down the street aways. Tell the feller that runs it that Charlie sent you and he'll set you right. Say I didn't get your name.'

'It's Laramie Davis,' Laramie said softly.

A small spark of recognition flickered in the barkeeps eyes. 'Glad to know you Mister Davis, like I said, your meal will be waitin' on your return.

He finished his beer, wiped foam from his top lip and walked outside to where the big Appaloosa awaited his owner. Laramie unwound the reins, then led Bo along the street to the livery stable. When he mentioned Charlie, the hostler seemed eager to help and was quite friendly. The straw filled stall for the night set him back two dollars, which included feed. Laramie passed him three and asked the man to have Bo ready for the trail early in the morning.

★ ★ ★

When he returned to the Red Eye Saloon, Charlie was true to his word and Laramie's meal waited for him. The plate was piled high with steak, potatoes, bacon and beans, topped with thick gravy.

'Find yourself a table, Mister Davis, and I'll bring you out another beer, or perhaps you'd prefer a pot of coffee?'

Charlie inquired.

'Beer will be fine, thanks Charlie. The meal looks mighty fine too.'

Charlie leaned in close and spoke softly, 'If you say anything I'll deny it but, my wife is the best damn cook in Montana.'

'I'll keep it under my hat.' Laramie smiled.

'You do that. Now go and find that table and I'll be right out.'

Laramie found a corner table from which he could watch the comings and goings through the batwings. Old habits, he thought.

Charlie was right about his wife being a great cook. The food was the best he'd eaten in a long while and he considered the possibility of an extra night. The steak was tender and the juices ran when he cut it. The potatoes tasted great, the bacon was crisp and the gravy was something else. When the apple pie came, and there were no words to describe how good it was. When Laramie paid for his meal, he slipped Charlie an extra two dollars.

He ordered a pot of coffee and sat back at his table. While he waited, a young man entered the saloon and walked up to the bar. He was of average height and build, had sandy coloured hair and wore black jeans and a blue shirt. His face appeared almost child-like with its fair skin. He seemed far too young to wear a tied down Colt at his right thigh. Laramie turned his attention to the badge pinned to the kid's breast pocket. Something told him that the kid was trouble, and he was right.

The kid called Charlie over and the two talked briefly before the young man turned to look in Laramie's direction. He adjusted his gun rig and weaved his way through the crowd to Laramie's table. Without an invitation, he sat down.

'Charlie tells me your name is Davis. My name is Jeremiah Coltrain. Deputy Jeremiah Coltrain,' he said and tapped the shiny nickel-plated badge.

Laramie studied him silently for a

moment, then asked warily, 'What can I do for you, Deputy?'

'Do you own that big Appaloosa stud down at the livery?' Coltrain asked.

Laramie nodded. 'I do.'

A broad smile split Coltrain's face. 'Great. How much do you want for him?'

Laramie was confused. He glanced towards the bar and saw Charlie with a concerned expression on his face. 'Are you telling me you want to buy my horse?'

The young man shook his head. 'No, I'm tellin' you I'm goin' to buy your horse.'

'Bo's not for sale Mister Coltrain.'

Coltrain laughed out loud. 'Everything is for sale at the right price Davis.'

'Not Bo. You don't have enough money, and even if you did I still wouldn't sell him.'

The glint of happiness left the young man's eyes and was replaced with a darkness that immediately put Laramie on edge. With a forced smile Coltrain said, 'I'm tryin' to be right polite about the sale I want to make Davis, but you ain't makin' it very easy. Now how things actually work around here is that I say I want to buy your horse and you say yes. Do you understand?'

Laramie stole another glance at Charlie who now sweated bullets. It was obvious that Coltrain had some sort of pull in town and Laramie guessed that he used the deputy's badge to wield it. As Laramie had been around for a long time, he would not be pushed by a punk kid. His voice held menace as he quietly said, 'Kid I already told you, Bo is not for sale. I strongly suggest that you get up and walk out of this saloon and let me finish my coffee.'

Coltrain's voice rose sharply as he leapt to his feet and knocked his chair backwards. 'Do you know who I am? What the name Coltrain means in this town?'

Laramie was aware of the sudden, heavy silence that descended in the Red Eye. Men closest to his table rose and moved away. 'No, kid. I don't know you from Adam, but I do know this. If you are thinkin' on pullin' that Colt your hand is restin' on I'd reconsider, because in the time it took for you to stand up I pulled and cocked one of my Remingtons. Right at this moment it's under this table pointed your way.'

Jeremiah Coltrain snorted derisively. 'You're bluffin', Davis.'

Laramie's voice remained calm, 'Are you willin' to die to find out?'

Coltrain stood still, uncertainty clouded his eyes. Laramie's words shook him some and he tried to figure out what to do next. In an attempt to salvage some dignity, he said stubbornly, 'I still mean to have that horse.'

And with that, he turned and stalked from the saloon.

Laramie watched the kid go and once through the bat wing doors, the noise level rose as everybody breathed a sigh of relief, but the look in the kid's eyes let him know that this wasn't over. Laramie eased the hammer down on the Remington and holstered it.

Twenty minutes later, the frantic hostler burst into the saloon and looked around until he found Laramie. He rushed up to the table and blurted out, 'Mister Davis, you'd best come quick. Jeremiah Coltrain is at your horse. He means to take him.'

'Damn fool kid,' Laramie cursed as he lurched to his feet and ran out of the saloon.

2

When Laramie arrived at the livery stable, Coltrain had Bo outside the large timber-framed doors, in an attempt to saddle him. Bo had other ideas. The appaloosa was a one-man horse and there was no way in hell he would let Jeremiah Coltrain ride him.

'Stand down Coltrain!' Laramie's voice sounded like a whip crack in the night. 'Let the horse go. I told you I wasn't sellin' him so if you let him go right now, you just might get away with the mistake of attempted horse stealing.'

Although the sun had gone down, the illumination of the lamp light from in the stables showed the bewilderment on Jeremiah Coltrain's face. 'You still don't get it, do you? We run this town. The Coltrain's run Rock Springs. What we say goes, and when I tell you I want this horse, I mean that I will have him. I offered you payment, but since you refused, I will just take him. Am I gettin' through to you yet?'

A crowd had gathered nearby and watched events unfold. Laramie had lost all patience with the kid and demanded, 'I said, let him go!'

Coltrain smiled and said coldly. 'Come and get him.'

Laramie moved like lightning. His left hand took hold of Bo's reins while his right hand made a fist and snaked out with unbelievable speed, and caught Coltrain flush on the jaw. The kid cried out, released the reins, and fell backward to the hard-packed earth. He lay there stunned, shook his head and tried to clear the cobwebs. When he wiped at the corner of his mouth, his hand came away red with blood.

'Damn you, you'll pay for that!' Coltrain snarled.

The deputy sheriff's hand flashed towards his holstered Colt. It had just cleared leather when Laramie's twin

Remingtons roared. Both shots punched into the kid's chest and killed him instantly. Laramie stood for a moment and looked at the young man he had just shot. It was senseless. A spoilt brat used to getting his own way, and now it had gotten him killed.

Laramie became aware of the man who stood beside him. 'Damn fool kid,' he muttered.

'That may be, Mister Davis,' Charlie the barkeep agreed, 'but you need to get gone from here now.'

'Why? It was self-defence. And the kid was tryin' to steal my horse.'

'Maybe so,' Charlie agreed again. 'But that boy's father is the town judge, his uncle is the town sheriff and his brother is a deputy. If you stay here they will certainly hang you before mornin'.'

A murmur rippled through the gathered crowd and Charlie called out, 'Chip, get the man's saddle and put it on his horse.'

The hostler ducked inside the stables

and returned with Laramie's saddle and Winchester, then immediately began to saddle the horse. Once finished, Laramie climbed up and turned to leave when a new voice cut through the noise of the crowd. 'Hold it right there, Mister.'

Laramie turned slightly in the saddle. In front of him stood the sheriff of Rock Springs, and in his fist, was a Colt .45.

'Hey, Uncle Jeb, it's Jeremiah,' Shell Coltrain gasped as he rushed forward.

Jebediah Coltrain gave no indication that he'd heard what Shell had said, 'Who are you, Mister?'

Laramie studied the man who stood in the false light of the stable's lanterns. Jebediah Coltrain was in his late forties and was a little under six feet tall. He had a solid build and greying hair, cold eyes and was dressed in denim pants, blue shirt and a calf skin vest.

'My name is Laramie Davis,' Laramie answered.

'The gunfighter?' the sheriff asked.

Laramie nodded.

'Uncle Jeb, Jeremiah's dead. The damn son of a bitch killed him. Shot him twice in the chest.'

'Looks like we're goin' to have us a hangin' in town,' Jeb Coltrain said without emotion.

A cold chill touched Laramie's spine as he explained, 'The kid was tryin' to steal my horse. When I tried to stop, him he went for his gun. It was a clear case of self-defence, Sheriff.'

'The stranger speaks the truth, Sheriff,' Charlie the barkeep said and backed Laramie's story. 'Young Jeremiah wanted his Appaloosa somethin' fierce and when the stranger said no, he tried to take it anyway. We were all here. Davis had no choice, Jeremiah would have shot him down.'

'Shut your yap, barkeep,' snapped Shell Coltrain savagely. 'He murdered my brother and for that he is goin' to pay with his life. An eye for an eye, right Uncle Jeb?'

The Sheriff nodded. 'I reckon so, Shell. You best run along and let your

18

father know about Jeremiah. I'll take care of this.'

Shell paused in the yellow light for a moment where Laramie could see him properly. He looked a lot like his dead brother, sandy hair, average build, maybe a little taller but he wore tailored clothes and held a Spencer carbine.

'Are you sure you don't want me to stick around?'

'Just go tell your Pa,' Jeb Coltrain snapped.

Laramie watched the young deputy leave then turned his attention back to the older Coltrain. 'You're makin' a big mistake, Sheriff.'

'The only mistake was made by you Davis, when you stopped in Rock Springs,' the sheriff pointed out. 'Now, are you goin' to climb down off that horse, or do I have to shoot you out of the saddle?'

Unnoticed by anyone, Charlie had slipped away from the crowd and stood by a stack of wooden crates. He pushed purposefully with his left hand which caused the crates to tumble, and as they hit the ground, several splintered.

The crash was a welcome distraction for Laramie as it caused the Sheriff's gaze to seek out the source of the disturbance. Laramie gave Bo a solid kick and the big horse leapt forward, his deep chest cannoned into the sheriff and knocked him from his feet. With a loud curse, Jeb Coltrain, although stunned, came to his feet and tried to line up his Colt with the fleeing rider's back as he escaped into the night. He fired three wild shots but missed with all, as the gunfighter rode low over the Appaloosa's neck. Jeb Coltrain managed to get another shot off before horse and rider disappeared.

The irate Sheriff turned his fury towards the worried townsfolk. 'When I find out which one of you helped that son of a bitch escape, I'll hang you on the scaffold next to him!'

'Make way, damn it, let me through.'

The crowd parted as an obese man of around fifty, dressed in black, forced his way through. His jowls wobbled and his cheeks flared as he puffed and panted from the exertion, 'Where is he? Where is the killer that murdered my boy?'

'He's gone, Judge,' Jeb Coltrain informed his brother.

'What? Where? How . . . How can he be gone?' Zebulon Coltrain asked, his confusion evident, 'Did you let him go? Shell said you had taken him prisoner.'

'No, I didn't damn well let him go,' he hissed, 'he escaped, and when I get to the bottom of it, he ain't goin' to be the only one swinging from a damn rope.'

'Where's my boy, Jeb?' the judge asked morosely.

The Sheriff pointed to where the body lay, 'Over there Zeb.'

The judge staggered on leaden legs towards his son's prone body and sank to his knees, a solitary figure, alone in his grief. A low keening escaped his lips, and continued for ten minutes until he rose to his feet, his face a mask of rage. 'I want him Jeb. I want that murdering bastard dead. Do you hear me? Dead! You form a posse right now and let's get after him.'

'Sure-thing Zeb, sure thing,' the sheriff said quietly and held his brother's gaze. 'Consider it done.'

3

Two days later, Blackie Harbin and his gang rode into Four Trails Way station a little before noon. So, named because of the stage trails that intersected there. The main trail ran from East to West, one from South-West terminated there, and the fourth trail ran due North. The way station sat on the West bank of the broad, fast flowing, Pine Tree River, and next to the rough pine log bridge that had been built in the station's early days of operation.

The country on the far side, rose sharply to the jagged mountains that formed the west wall of Pine Tree River Valley. The lower slopes were covered with Fir trees and Ponderosa Pines, a smattering of other species mixed throughout, as well as large boulders shaped like giant marbles. The river, shallow at this point, had rocks which jutted above the surface amidst a roiling mass of white water.

The construction of the station was logs from the surrounding forest, hand tooled and slotted together. Mud was used to create a weather proof finish. The adjacent corral used the slimmer lodge pole pines, and a rough plank barn sat at the rear.

Animals grazed in the lush meadow that was spotted with small yellow wild flowers. In the station yard, a Concorde stage with a team of six horses in the traces, stood and waited. Emblazoned on the stage's side, in yellow writing was, *North-West Stage Lines*. Four men lay dead on the ground, flies buzzed around the bullet holes and fed on the not yet congealed blood.

Beside the stage stood a young woman, her sky-blue dress crumpled from the journey. Next to her was a travelling salesman, who stood transfixed with his arms raised, his brow soaked in sweat. Fear coursed through him as he stared down the barrels of the four guns pointed at him.

He swallowed hard and stammered, 'P . . . P . . . Please don't shoot me. I have a family. I won't say anything, I swear it.'

An outlaw smiled coldly, his blackened teeth showing, and said, 'You're damn right there,' and took up the slack on the trigger and the hammer fell. His gun roared, the thunderous sound reverberated from the surrounding peaks. The salesman was thrown back as the .45 calibre bullet took him in the chest. He landed heavily in the dirt, twitched once and died.

The woman screamed, her brown eyes wide and filled with tears.

'Chris, take her inside. I'll work out what to do with her later.'

'Sure, Blackie,' Chris answered, with a hint of expectation of what was to come.

Blackie Harbin and his gang were the scourge of the North-West. Harbin was the worst. The outlaw was tall and thin, with shoulder length black hair, and brown, hate filled eyes, set in a square jawed face. He favoured a duster coat and denim pants, twin, pearl handled Colts strapped around his slim waist. He ran his gang with an iron fist and showed no mercy toward any man who questioned his decisions.

There were six outlaws in all. Harbin, Chris, Cato, Slate, Benny and Lone Wolf and each of them was wanted by the law.

Chris, at twenty-five, was five eight tall, had black hair and a solid build. His beady grey eyes were set deep in his tanned face.

Cato was thirty-two and of similar build to Chris. He was wiry but had sandy hair and blue eyes.

Slate was a recent addition to Harbin's gang. He was twenty-five and stood six feet in his socks. His hair and eyes were brown and his face was hawkish. Slate had been a petty criminal until he'd met the outlaw leader.

Benny was a baby-faced killer. He

was twenty-one, slim built with blond hair and blue eyes. He dressed in black and wore twin Peacemakers. He was what the old hands called a wannabe.

That just left Lone Wolf, who was Crow Indian with all the Indian traits. He was tough and wiry and stood five ten. He was quiet, spoke only when spoken to, most of the time, but when riled, turned into an efficient killer.

As Chris dragged the young woman into the stage station by her long, black hair, Cato and Slate approached Blackie with the strong box they'd found under one of the Concorde's seats. 'Here it is Blackie, they had it stashed away.'

'Take it inside, but shoot that damn lock off before you do,' the outlaw leader ordered.

The two men dropped the box on the hard-packed earth with a dull thud. Cato drew his Colt and there was a triple click as he eared back the hammer. It was followed by the loud boom of the shot as he blew the lock off the heavy, iron-strapped strong box, then picked it up and carried it inside.

'Benny,' Harbin called out to the youngest one, 'you and Lone Wolf keep watch, I don't want any surprises.'

'Sure Blackie, whatever you say.'

Harbin turned on his heel and followed the others inside.

★   ★   ★

Laramie Davis sat on his haunches under a tall Ponderosa Pine, his broad back leant up against the rough bark of its trunk. Bo was ground hitched further back in the trees and remained out of sight.

He had watched the stage station for a good while and observed the sickening, cold blooded murder of the salesman, the woman dragged by her hair, and the heavy lock box go off in the same direction.

Laramie had become aware that he was riding into trouble when the pop-pop of gunshots reached him as he rode steadily along the trail. Those shots had killed the driver, the shotgun guard and an extra guard hired for the money transport.

When the shots had first rung out, Laramie eased Bo off the trail and into the surrounding stands of Ponderosa. His nose filled with the scent of the pine as he climbed down from his Mexican saddle and crept forward to get a better view. One thing he'd learned in his forty-five years, was that you don't rush into a situation you know nothing about.

From his vantage point, he'd seen all he needed, to know what had happened and now there was a choice to make. Become involved, or ride far around and keep ahead of the posse that dogged his trail.

'Oh hell,' Laramie said as he stood up and stretched out the kinks. 'We all gotta die someday.'

★　★　★

Ten miles to the East, in a patch of rocky ground off the main trail, a tall

Blackfoot warrior looked down upon the lifeless bodies of his brother and brother's wife. The rage slowly built in Black Elk and a slight tremble was, for the moment, the only outward sign. Judging by the tracks, Lame Bear and Lost Dove had been ambushed by six men. His brother had been shot three times in an attempt to protect his wife. Lost Dove had not been so lucky. The beautiful young Indian woman, with flawless skin, had been abused by her killers until her torment was ended by a slash to her throat.

Black Elk walked methodically around the horrific scene, and studied all the sign. The afternoon sun beat down on his muscular frame as he bent on one knee and gently touched the earth where Lost Dove's blood had seeped into the soil. He gathered some dirt, and rubbed it between his fingers. The pair had been killed early that morning he decided. Black Elk stood and wiped his fingers on his deerskin breeches, his eyes followed the trail of the long-gone riders.

The time for grief would come later. Revenge was foremost in his mind as he began to gather up the bodies and return them to his camp. With a large group of his warriors, he would then hunt down these evil men and kill them very slowly.

★   ★   ★

Laramie rode in on the trail from the South-West. He swayed easily with the big Appaloosa's gait as it picked the way along the trail. Bo had been given to him by a Cheyenne warrior some time back. Laramie had helped save him from a blood hungry group of settlers who'd sought the justice of lynch law. When asked what the crime was, the leader of the maddened group could only reason that he was, 'Indian'.

As Laramie rode into the station yard, he found himself confronted by the Indian, Lone wolf and the baby-faced killer, Benny. Both barred his way with raised Winchesters.

'Who are you Mister?' challenged Benny.

'Who wants to know?' Laramie asked belligerently.

'I do,' came Benny's short reply.

Laramie shrugged. 'Just a stranger passin' through.'

Benny ran a careful eye over the gunfighter. He was unsure on what to do next. This man didn't look like a normal stranger passin' through.

'You fellers look like you've had some trouble here,' Laramie observed as he nodded at the bodies stretched out on the ground.

Benny smiled coldly. 'Nothin' we couldn't handle.

Laramie's tone hardened when next he spoke, 'How about you fellers get those saddle guns out of my face.'

Not one to take a backward step, Benny replied, 'How about I just shoot you.'

'That's enough,' Harbin's voice was a harsh rasp. 'Don't you dimwits know greatness when you see it?'

Benny spat in the dirt. 'All I see is a bum on horseback.'

'This 'bum' as you called him,' Harbin informed Benny, 'just happens to be Laramie Davis, the second fastest gun in the territory.'

'You'd be the fastest, Blackie?' asked Laramie.

Harbin smiled, 'Of course.'

Laramie indicated the stiffening bodies on the ground. 'I see you've been hard at work.'

Harbin shrugged nonchalantly. 'One of the hazards of the job.'

'Let me shoot him Blackie,' Benny said gleefully.

'Shut your whinin', boy,' Harbin snarled. 'Take the man's horse and put it in the corral. When you've done that, get rid of those bodies before they start stinkin' up the place.'

Laramie climbed down and let Benny have his horse.

'Treat him careful boy,' Laramie warned, 'I'm kinda partial to that animal. I'd hate for anything to happen to him.'

Laramie turned his attention back to Harbin. 'It's been a long time Blackie.'

'Sure has Laramie,' Harbin agreed. 'You've changed some.'

'A little older,' Laramie allowed, 'but, I see you ain't changed any.'

Harbin's eyes glittered wickedly. 'Nope, I sure ain't. So, you'd best remember that.'

Laramie let the open challenge go and nodded in acknowledgement.

'Anyway,' Harbin eased the tension in the air, 'Chris is cookin' some grub. Maybe you're hungry.'

The two men walked into the station. Laramie let his eyes adjust to the lower light and with a gaze that had kept him alive this long, took in everything before him.

The main room was a large, open area that held timber dining tables and chairs. A small bar was built against the far wall and a large fireplace, surrounded by wooden panels, would fill the room with sufficient heat to ward off the chill of the cold winters that occurred here in the mountains. There were four doors that led off the main area, and all were closed. Laramie guessed three were rooms while the fourth would be, hopefully, a back way out. Hidden away in a corner, was a large wood stove, where a man stood and cooked.

At a table with a check table cloth, sat two other men. They each had a shot glass of whiskey in front of them, and both men stared at Laramie.

Recognition flared in the face of one. 'Ahh shoot, howdy Laramie.'

'Howdy Slate, what are you doin' ridin' with this pack of no goods?' Laramie inquired. The last he knew of Slate was that he had settled down from his petty outlaw days, and gone back to earning an honest living.

'Yeah, well,' Slate shrugged, 'the whole workin' hard for a livin' didn't work out. You know how it is. What are you doin' around here?'

'Headin' for Canada,' Laramie answered honestly.

'Are things getting' too hot for you? The great Laramie Davis,' Harbin's sarcasm hung heavily in the air.

'I shot a Sheriff's deputy,' Laramie reluctantly explained. 'It was self-defence but his father was the local judge and the family was set on hangin' me.'

Unable to contain his amusement, Blackie Harbin laughed out loud. It sounded more like a donkey braying than anything human. 'Well, well, welcome to the other side.'

The seriousness of the situation penetrated Harbin's moment of happiness and a darkness fell across his face. 'Son of a . . . did you bring a God damned posse down on us Laramie?' Harbin exploded. 'If you have I'll kill you right now!'

'Calm down,' said Laramie reassuringly, and he tried to ease the tension that had developed with his admission. 'I lost the posse yesterday.'

Blackie eased his hand away from the butt of the Colt on his left side. 'Just as well.'

One of the closed doors squeaked open, and through it walked the woman from the stage. She had changed her clothes. The blue dress had gone and had been replaced by denim pants and a man's cotton shirt, which was tucked in and accentuated the curves of her slim body. She walked silently and swiftly to a vacant table, as far removed from the others as she could get.

'Food's ready,' Chris called from over by the stove.

It was the first time that Laramie had noticed the aroma which drifted across the room, and he thought to himself that it smelled good.

'About time,' Harbin said.

Laramie watched as the outlaws grabbed tin plates and slopped stew onto them. He looked across at the woman and noticed that she hadn't moved. She showed no indication that the call for food even reached her.

'Are you eatin' or what Mister Legend?' Chris asked from beside the stove.

Laramie nodded and grabbed two tin plates and held them out for the outlaw to fill. He filled the first plate but left the second empty and challenged Laramie with a stare.

'Fill it,' Laramie said flatly.

'You only need one,' Chris pointed out and remained unmoved.

'It's for the lady. Now fill it,' Laramie said and gave Chris a withering stare.

The outlaw shrugged and filled the plate, and in the process slopped a little of the hot food on Laramie's hand. 'Sorry,' he apologised. 'Missed it.'

Laramie, let it go, found two relatively clean forks, and turned away from the grinning outlaw. He took both plates to where the woman was seated and sat down. He nudged one of the plates towards her with a fork.

She looked Laramie squarely in the eye and said with open hostility, 'I'm not hungry.'

'You best eat Miss, you'll probably be needin' it,' Laramie said softly.

Frustrated, the woman said, 'I told

you, I'm not hungry.'

'Is our company not good enough for you, Mister Legend?' It was Benny. He'd come inside from his chores, having buried the dead, sat at a table with the others, and wolfed down his stew.

Laramie ignored the barb Benny threw at him and continued to eat his surprisingly tasty stew.

'Didn't you hear me Legend?' Benny asked around a mouthful of his meal. 'Ain't we good enough for the likes of you. Or maybe us big, bad outlaws scare the pants off you.'

Laramie lifted his gaze to the woman who sat across from him. Her worried expression pleaded with him not to start anything. He nodded almost imperceptibly and it was enough to relieve some of her tension.

Benny couldn't help himself and continued to push. 'You know what fellers? I think this old has been is yeller!'

Every person in the Four Trails way station put down their forks, except for Laramie. The others waited for the gunman to stand and take up the kid's challenge. Instead, Laramie said coolly, 'Blackie, you'd best tell that young pup to back off before his mouth digs his grave.'

'Why you . . . ' Benny lunged to his feet. His chair skidded back and fell as he clawed at one of his Peacemakers. As he drew, a shot thundered, the sound loud and deafening as it bounced off the timber walls. Benny's gun tumbled to the floor and he grabbed at the bloody furrow, the bullet from Harbin's Colt had gouged out.

'If I want him dead boy, I'll do the shootin',' Blackie Harbin growled in a low voice, as he held a smoking gun. 'Not you. Just you keep that in mind.'

'Damn Blackie, you shot me,' Benny whined

'The next time I shoot you will be for keeps.'

The woman sat horrified as she watched Laramie casually continue to eat his stew.

No one saw that Slate had drawn his

gun under the table, and had it pointed in Benny's direction.

After Harbin slid his gun back into its well-oiled holster, he leaned close to the table and spoke quietly, 'You boys keep an eye on him. He's up to somethin'. I know it and before we leave here tomorrow I want him dead.'

'You best eat up Miss, before your meal goes cold,' Laramie said, and calmly showed no outward sign of concern for the situation.

'Who are you?' The woman finally asked, overcoming her shock.

'The name's Laramie Davis, Miss,' he answered her question.

She mulled his name over in her mind for a moment before realisation finally came.

'I know your name,' she gasped. 'You're that Gunman, that killer.'

'Some have called me that,' he allowed. 'Others a lot worse.'

She was amazed he could talk like that, like it didn't matter. 'You are no better than they are.'

For some reason the barb from the woman stung, but he did not let it show. She obviously didn't realise that he was able to help her. 'Miss the way I see it, you have two choices. You can stay with these outlaws who will eventually kill you, after they've had their fun.' he paused for a moment and let his words sink in, 'Or you can trust me and maybe we will both get out of this alive. Just remember this before you decide. I rode in here because I saw what happened to those men they murdered. I could have ridden on, but I didn't.'

'Why should I trust you?'

'Seems to me you don't have much choice, Miss.'

The young lady sighed resignedly. 'If I'm to put my life in your hands, you may as well know my name. It's Sally Richards.'

Laramie smiled warmly. 'So, where are you from Sally Richards?'

'Mountain Pass,'

'Say, you're Pa wouldn't be Hank

42

Richards, would it?' Laramie asked, surprised.

'Yes, it is,' Sally confirmed.

'Is he still town Sheriff?'

'Yes, but how did you know that?' Sally asked, a confused look on her face.

'The old days Miss. We rode together some before he decided to settle down and take good care of his family,' Laramie explained.

Sally looked indignant, 'My father was a United States Marshal, not some common gunman.'

'Yes Miss, he was,' Laramie agreed. 'So was I.'

'You were a Marshal?' Sally asked in disbelief.

'Sure was,' Laramie confirmed.

'I'll vouch for that Miss,' neither one of them had noticed Slate approach the table, 'then he added quickly, 'I need to talk to you later Laramie. Outside, after dark.'

Laramie didn't answer, but gave a slight incline of his head. Slate moved on and left Laramie to ponder on his words.

Silence descended over the table.

4

The afternoon progressed to early evening. The sun dropped behind the mountains and day slowly turned into night. Stars sparkled like diamonds in the sky and the large moon cast its silvery glow over the landscape, and thus kept the night from total darkness.

Inside the way station, all the outlaws lounged around, except for Benny. He sat on a chair, a scowl on his face directed at Laramie. The gunman knew the time would come that he would have to kill the kid. He just didn't know when the move would be made.

After the evening meal of leftover stew, Laramie excused himself from the table he sat at with Sally and walked towards the door which led outside. The audible triple click of a gun hammer being thumbed back sounded loud in the confines of the station house. 'Where do you think you're goin' Laramie?'

The gunfighter froze, then turned and faced Harbin. 'I'm goin' to check on my horse.'

Harbin shook his head. 'Nope. You stay right here. Benny put it in the corral, it's fine.'

'If you're worried about me runnin' off, why don't you send a man along to keep me company. Besides when I leave here, I'm takin' the lady with me.'

'That's mighty big talk for a man faced with six guns,' Harbin pointed out.

'Maybe so,' Laramie agreed, 'but I have two six-guns, each with six shots. That's twelve bullets. Now I probably won't get all six of you but that won't worry you none, because you'll be dead first.'

Laramie's hands edged closer to his Remingtons. 'You decide Blackie, but make it quick, I ain't got all day.'

Tension in the room built and Harbin licked his lips. The outlaw's gun was out and cocked but Laramie's calmness in the face of death, had unnerved him.

'I'll go and keep an eye on him Blackie,' Slate's voice broke the tension.

It was the out Harbin needed, and he eased down the hammer on his gun. 'Fine Slate, you go. But don't be out there too long.'

'No problem,' Slate said and followed Laramie out the door.

Outside the clear night air had a crisp feel about it and pricked the exposed skin of both men. Once they were away from the building, Slate said in bewilderment. 'Damn, Laramie, were you tryin' to get yourself killed in there.'

'Don't worry none about that,' the gunfighter said and looked about to see if they were alone. 'What did you want to talk to me about?'

Slate sighed and informed him, 'They're goin' to kill you before they leave tomorrow.'

'Why are you tellin' me this?' Laramie enquired.

'I'm thinkin' if I help you, you can help me,' Slate explained a little.

Laramie's interest was piqued. 'How do I get to help you.'

'I need to get away from Harbin,' he said. 'The man is crazy. He just kills and kills and he don't stop. You ever seen the look in his eye when he does it? He enjoys it. Most of them do. That damn Benny, I swear he's Harbin's kid. He gets the same look. I just gotta get away from 'em Laramie.'

Laramie listened in silence and thought before he answered. He looked at Slate and saw the pleading in his eyes and realised that he may come in handy when it was time. 'Alright Slate we'll do it your way.'

Slate's relief was obvious as his face came to life. 'Your best opportunity to escape will be tonight while I'm on watch. If you can get out, I'll have horses ready and we'll be gone well and truly before they wake up.'

'Make sure you are ready,' Laramie said seriously, 'because if Blackie and his boys wake up, we'll need to shoot our way out.'

'Don't worry, we'll be ready.'

Laramie checked on Bo, and the Appaloosa crossed to him and nuzzled his hand as he held it out to rub the horse's nose. 'Hang in there big feller, it won't be long now. We'll be gone come mornin' and I'll be needin' everythin' you have.'

*   *   *

Amongst the cedar and cottonwoods, beside a fast-flowing creek, the posse had made camp for the night. In the wilderness surrounding their camp, a Grey Wolf's low, mournful howl made the horses fidget nervously at their tethers.

'Whoa, horses,' soothed Orson Blake. 'He's just callin' to his friends. He don't want to eat you tonight. Might take a chunk out of old Grover over there though.'

'That ain't funny Orson,' grouched

Grover Yates, the oldest man in the posse. 'I heard tell about a bunch of trappers once, camped up in these mountains. They left a feller on watch one night and when they woke up the next mornin' he was gone. All they found was a bunch of wolf tracks and his old Hawken rifle.'

Orson Blake laughed at the old store owner. 'And you actually believe that story Grover?'

'It's a true story Orson, it was told to me by one of them mountain men personally,' Grover said, indignant that Orson would make fun of the tale.

Jebediah Coltrain stalked out of the darkness and stopped in front of the two posse men, 'When you two are finished with your bed time stories, you might want to keep watch. We ain't the only ones out here you know, or did you forget the Indian pony tracks we came across this afternoon?'

'Sure thing sheriff,' mumbled Orson Blake. 'We'll get right back to it.'

'And damned well stay awake. I don't

want to be wakin' up in the middle of the night with some savage redskin standin' over me holdin' my hair in his hand.' Coltrain ordered.

Jeb left them to it and strode back into camp where the rest of the posse were camped out. There were seven men who formed the judge's vengeance posse; not all of them willing. There was the judge, Jeb Coltrain, Shell Coltrain and Jim Clancy. Orson Blake and Grover Yates were on watch, while the seventh man, Clay Adams, stirred the fire under the coffee pot.

'Don't go makin' that fire too big Clay,' cautioned Jeb Coltrain. 'Don't want to be givin' away our position to any of them redskins floatin' around out there.'

Clay grabbed a handful of dirt and threw it on the orange flames to damp them down some. He was a thin, young cow hand from one of the ranches that surrounded Rock Springs. He happened to be in the wrong place at the right time and got pushed into a posse against his will. He wasn't alone. Grover and Orson were in the same boat.

Jim Clancy, on the other hand, was a gunman. He was tall and willowy, was in his early thirties, and wore his dark hair collar length. His grey eyes moved constantly. He worked for the Coltrains when they paid him for it. He wasn't fussy, especially when the price was right.

'What was that you said?' Zeb Coltrain asked his brother. 'Did you see more Indian sign out there?'

The Sheriff shook his head. 'Nope, didn't see a thing, except two no good greenhorns lookin' the wrong damned way. Don't mean they ain't out there though.'

'So is that filthy murderer who killed my boy,' snapped the judge.

'We'll pick up his trail tomorrow Zeb. We know he's headin' towards the border,' the sheriff spoke matter of factly.

The judge struggled to his feet and

looked his brother hard in the eyes, his flabby jowls quivered with pent up rage. 'I don't care if the killer gets across the damn border into Canada. We will not stop until he is dead. Do you understand?'

The judge looked around the group and lay down the challenge. 'Do you all understand? When you rode out of Rock Springs you signed on until the end,' he reached inside his coat pocket and pulled out his imported Webley Bulldog pocket revolver. 'I will damn well shoot any man who tries to back out!'

'Ease up Judge,' Jeb cautioned. 'No man's backin' out. You keep that up and we'll be buryin' you next.'

The big man put his gun away and sat down. 'Just you make sure they don't'

'We'll ride to Four Trails swing station tomorrow, Judge,' Jeb explained to his brother. 'He'll have to ride through there to get to the border. Besides, he can't hide forever. That damn horse of his is a dead giveaway. We should reach there sometime in the morning, of course that depends on how much them damn townsfolk slow us down.'

Judge Zebulon Coltrain gave no indication that he'd heard his brother's last words. He just sat and stared at the orange flames of the camp fire as it flickered in the dark and licked hungrily at the small branches that fed its being. The fire would slowly devour the wood just as the burning hatred in the judge would eventually consume him.

★   ★   ★

One by one, the outlaws at Four Trails fell into a deep slumber, helped along by the contents of three bottles of whiskey from behind the bar. Laramie watched them intently from under the brim of his dark coloured Stetson as they dropped off.

It was almost midnight, and Lone Wolf and Slate had been on watch for three hours. At one point, Laramie had thought that not all the outlaws would give in to the peaceful murmurings of sleep.

The sandy headed Cato was the last to succumb and it wasn't long before his soft snore joined the chorus of the others.

With a small sigh of relief, Laramie eased his feet from the chair they rested on and slowly tilted the Stetson back so he could see more clearly in the low glow of the lantern light. He sat up and cautiously looked for any indication that the outlaws were aware of his movements.

None of them stirred, so Laramie, careful to make no noise, stood up and waited before he moved. Stealthily he crept towards the door which Sally waited behind nervously.

Laramie tried the handle and it turned easily. He pushed the door open and slipped through the narrow gap. He closed the door and the latch clicked shut. He heard Sally expel an anxious breath.

'Thank God it's you Laramie,' she whispered. 'I was beginning to think you weren't coming.'

Laramie placed a hand on her arm to quiet her. 'When we leave, the only way to go is through that main area where the outlaws are sleeping. Try to be as quiet as possible. If anything goes bad, run out the door and don't look back. Slate will get you away from here.'

'What about you?' The concern was clear in her hushed tone.

'Don't worry about me. Slate will have horses ready. You get on one and don't stop until you are well clear of here. He will take you to your father.'

'Okay.'

'Are you ready?' he asked.

'Yes,' Sally answered apprehensively.

Laramie's voice grew grim. 'Follow me.'

He stood before the door and took a deep breath, then dropped his hand to one of his Remingtons, drew it from its holster, and thumbed back the hammer. It was hard to tell which was louder, the triple click of the gun, or the sound of his breath, as both seemed thunderous in the darkness.

Laramie levelled his hand gun and once more opened the door. It gave a slight squeak and to his ears, it sounded like someone had dropped an armful of pots and pans on the floor. He froze when one of the outlaws stirred, Cato he thought, or maybe Chris. He waited uneasily for whom ever it was, to return to sleep. He eased forward through the doorway and out into the main room of the way station. Sally was close behind, and he prayed silently under his breath that nothing would happen to endanger her life.

They reached the halfway point of the room, Laramie now acutely aware of any changes in the outlaw's breathing patterns. Benny snorted, moaned and mumbled something incoherent. There was a small gasp from Sally, and the gunfighter hoped she could hold her nerve. He watched as Benny rolled over, then continued his soft snores.

The pair moved on and finally reached the door that led outside. Laramie's hand touched the door handle and paused before he turned it. The handle turned silently and he eased the door open with a grimace. No alarm was sounded.

With his arm around Sally, the gunfighter guided her through the door first, then followed, and shut it gently behind them.

Laramie belatedly remembered something that caused a small flash of alarm in him. Lone Wolf, the Crow Indian, was on watch, somewhere out there in the darkness. He hoped like hell that Slate had managed to take care of him.

*   *   *

Slate had indeed taken care of the Indian and Lone Wolf was now laid out and trussed in the barn behind the corral. He saddled the horses they would need for their flight, and settled in to wait for Laramie and the woman.

After what seemed an eternal wait,

and the hope that none of the other outlaws or even Blackie himself would emerge, Slate started to lose hope and thought seriously about making a run for it. He figured he'd ride east, far away from where he was now, and far away from any living soul who knew him.

Two figures moved past the corral towards the barn. Slate tensed for a moment and then realised it was Laramie and the woman.

'About time you two turned up,' Slate said softly, relief evident. 'I was gettin' set to ride without you. Didn't think you were comin'.'

'It took your friends in there a while to get to sleep,' Laramie explained. 'Where is Lone Wolf?'

'I have him tucked away in the barn. He won't be gettin' free any time soon.'

The gunfighter nodded. 'Good. Right then, let's put some distance between us and here before the others wake up and work out somethin' is wrong.'

Slate had the horses ready behind the barn. Bo gave a low nicker when Laramie neared and the gunfighter gave the big horse a reassuring rub on his muscular neck.

'I hope they don't wake up while we're riding out of here,' Sally voiced her concerns.

'We'll lead the horses until we're out of earshot, then mount up,' Laramie explained to Sally.

As quietly as possible, they led the three horses out of the barn and past the corral. Once clear, Laramie gave Slate Bo's reins and whispered, 'Keep goin', I'll let their horses out to give us more of an advantage.'

While the others disappeared into the darkness, Laramie dropped the two Lodge Pole rails used as a gate. The horses milled about skittishly, unused to the strange man who walked among them. Once inside the corral, he gently urged the horses toward the opening, careful not to spook them, and keep noise to a minimum. They walked through the opening and out into the meadow.

Laramie caught up with Sally and Slate in the tree line that circled the meadow. 'Where to now?' Slate asked him.

'Into the mountains,' he answered.

Sally was a little surprised by this. 'Why? Why the mountains? Shouldn't we take the trail and try to get to Mountain Pass?'

'We *are* goin' to Mountain Pass, Sally,' Laramie answered truthfully. 'But we're takin' the long way around. From here, I mean to go to Beaver Meadow. Don't forget I'm bein' followed by that posse from Rock Springs. If Blackie comes after us, which I think he will, I want to try to lose them all in the mountains. If they flounder around lookin' for our trail, all the better for us. Now stop gabbin' and get on your horses.'

* * *

61

Two hours before dawn, a man stepped from of the tree line close to Four Trails way station, closely followed by another.

'Are you sure they are here?' the first man asked.

'I am sure.'

The first man stared at the way station and grunted a reply. Both men stood and watched in silence for a short while before they melted quietly back into the trees.

5

'Get up!' roared Blackie Harbin as he kicked Cato savagely in the ribs. 'Why in hell are you not on watch?'

Cato struggled to sit up, and held his side where Harbin had delivered the blow. 'What the hell Blackie? What did you do that for?'

The others started to stir, and Benny asked through his waking fog. 'What's goin' on Blackie?'

'What's goin' on Blackie?' The furious outlaw leader mimicked. 'I'll tell you what's goin' on! You and this damned lunk head here were meant to be on watch hours ago. Instead, I wake up and find you still asleep in here. Not to mention, Laramie and the damn woman have gone!'

This last statement snapped all the outlaws wide awake. 'How could they be gone?' asked Chris warily.

'Because they damn well had help,' Harbin fumed. 'When I woke up and saw Davis gone, I checked on the woman and found her gone too! Then I went outside and guess what? Slate was gone too! As were the horses! After that, I found Lone Wolf tied up in the barn!'

Cato, Chris and Benny remained silent; they thought it best, under the circumstances. With Blackie's mood the way it was, there was a good chance he would shoot someone.

Harbin's rant continued, 'So right at this point in time Lone Wolf is lookin' for sign as to which way they went. What you three are goin' to do, is get our damn horses back that they let go! Now get the hell out there!'

The outlaws snatched up their weapons and filed quickly out the door, eager to escape their boss's wrath. Harbin followed close behind. Half way across the station yard, Lone wolf jogged in, concern etched on his normally impassive face.

'Hold them up Blackie,' he said hurriedly. 'Get them back inside, now!'

Harbin was confused. 'Why? We need them horses back. They lost 'em and they can damn well get them back.'

'There's Blackfeet in the trees,' the Crow explained rapidly. 'We need to be back inside.'

Before Harbin could speak, a soft whistle filled the air followed by a dull thunk as a Blackfoot arrow hit Chris in the chest. The outlaw looked down in bewilderment at the protrusion that he had sprouted. He looked up at Cato. 'Damn Cato, I think I'm dead.'

Chris' knees folded and he fell to the ground.

A dozen Blackfoot warriors emerged swiftly from the trees, and caught the outlaws unprepared. More arrows rained down, but narrowly missed targets. Harbin was the first to react. 'Take cover, damn it! Don't stand around gapin' at him, he's dead.'

Harbin brought up his six-guns and cut loose. The Blackfeet scattered as one of their number went down wounded, a crimson patch stood out against his skin.

The outlaws slowly retreated toward the cover of the station house. Benny had both his Colts out, and worked them methodically. The Indians soon found good cover, and after the loss of the first brave, the outlaws found it difficult to find a target.

Lone Wolf shouted a warning above the gun fire and Harbin turned. The Crow pointed at something behind the corral. There were almost two dozen more Blackfeet, but these were armed with rifles. Whilst the outlaw's attention had been drawn by the direct attack in front, the others had slipped out of the thick forest behind them.

Hell, thought Harbin before he called out to the others at the top of his voice, 'Get back inside! The devils are behind us too.'

The outlaws turned to face the new threat. The air was instantly filled with the snap of bullets that passed close.

One tugged at Harbin's sleeve, while another made a red furrow along Cato's arm, and caused him to cry out in pain.

The outlaws immediately ceased fire and hurriedly made for the way station's main door. Benny wasn't so quick to retreat. The kid had a hero complex and thought that he was invincible, bulletproof. A bullet nicked his thigh. Not enough to disable him, but enough to cause pain and make Benny realise that perhaps he wasn't immortal after all.

The kid was hot on Blackie Harbin's heels when the outlaw leader dived through the doorway. The tough hard-wood door slammed shut and the locking bar was thrust across and wedged in place.

Glass shattered as the outlaws took up positions by the windows. Rifle barrel's poked through and started to bark.

'Cato, how's that arm of yours?' Harbin shouted over the din.

Cato kept firing and said, 'Flesh

wound Blackie, I'll worry about it later.'

'Good, you and Lone Wolf watch the back. Make sure it's secure.'

Without a word Cato and the Crow, hurried across to the other side of the building and into rooms at the rear. It wasn't long before their guns fired again, and held the attack from that side at bay.

Harbin reloaded his rifle and sneaked a glance around the corner of the window frame. The Indians were closer now and some were in the yard. One Indian rose from behind a water trough and loosed an arrow which embedded itself in the outside wall only inches from the window frame Harbin was at. It caused him to flinch as he ducked back and cursed out loud.

'God damn Redskins, what the hell are they doin' here?'

'I'll give you one guess?' Benny answered.

'Yeah, well let's see if we can kill us some more.'

Harbin thrust his rifle back through

the broken window pane and fired another volley of shots. Two Indians went down in a heap out in the open. One didn't move, but the other writhed in pain, which only ceased when a bullet from Benny's rifle mercifully ended his suffering.

Benny shifted his aim and fired at a warrior who approached from the right. The Brave cried out and through the gun smoke, Benny watched him go down clutching at his middle. After Blackie wounded another one, the Blackfeet pulled back behind cover and into the trees.

The gunfire from inside the way station died off and all went quiet. The main room was filled with the blue grey mist of gun smoke and the smell of burnt powder.

Outside, Harbin could see at least six unmoving warriors on the ground. Who knew how many wounded had gotten away. He looked around and saw a rivulet of blood that coursed down the side of Benny's face. 'Are you okay kid?'

Benny wiped the side of his face and

saw blood as his hand came away. 'Yeah, just a scratch. A bullet came through the window and caught some glass left in the frame, smashed it and a splinter must have nicked me.'

Harbin then noticed the wet patch of blood on the thigh of Benny's black pants. 'What about that?'

Benny shrugged nonchalantly.

'Keep an eye out, I'll see how the others are farin',' Harbin said.

Blackie checked on Lone Wolf who was fine, and resolutely guarded his window. When he checked on Cato, he found that he also, held vigil at a window.

'How's the arm?' Blackie asked, he'd noticed red on the shirt sleeve.

'Hurts like a bitch but once we get a bit more time, I'll patch it up proper.'

'How many do you figure are out back here?' Harbin asked.

Cato wasn't sure. 'I think we took care of four or so, but if I had to hazard a guess, I would say maybe fifteen or sixteen are left.'

Harbin nodded thoughtfully. 'Well

one thing's for sure, they got us surrounded.'

'You know why they're here don't you?' said Cato.

Harbin nodded but before he could speak, Benny's voice called out in alarm, 'They're comin' again Blackie.'

Benny's rifle started its deadly work once more.

The outlaw boss smiled coldly. 'And here I was hopin' they was goin' to give up. Keep your head down Cato.'

'How are we goin' to get out of this one, Blackie?' Cato asked, concerned.

Harbin called over his shoulder on the way out of the small room, 'Hell, just hope they run out of Indians before we run out of bullets.'

★   ★   ★

It was a faint sound, carried on the morning breeze up the valley between the two snow-capped mountains. Laramie pulled back on Bo's reins and the big horse eased to a stop beside a large outcrop of granite. Sally and Slate stopped their mounts as well.

'What's up?' Slate asked, curious as to why they had stopped.

Laramie held up his finger for them both to stay quiet. His ears strained to pick out the sound again, but his persistence was rewarded. 'There, did you hear that?'

Slate nodded slowly, unsure. He'd heard something but didn't know what.

'There it is again,' confirmed the gunfighter.

'I heard it that time,' Slate agreed.

'Heard what?' Sally asked, confused.

'Gunfire,' explained Slate.

'What do you make of it?' Laramie asked.

'Do you think it's coming from Four Trails?' asked Slate.

Laramie took off his hat and ran a hand through his brown hair before he replaced it, 'Could be,' he allowed. 'But I don't plan on goin' back to find out.'

Laramie heeled Bo forward and the horse responded smoothly. Sally and the outlaw, Slate followed behind.

Eventually the trio entered a valley, one of many in this part of the mountains, not too distant from Four Trails. It was narrow and filled with immense stands of Ponderosa and Douglas fir. At its end, where the valley narrowed to what seemed to be a triangle point, the trail climbed up to a pass named after a French trapper who'd worked the area in the early eighteen twenties. None of the mountain men of the time could pronounce his name properly so the pass just became known as Frenchie's.

From there, the trail dropped down into another valley which was a vast expanse of meadows and streams. A small lake sat on the valley's south side surrounded by various vegetation that included, Fir trees, Red Cedar and Western Hemlock. Elk and Mule deer were prevalent and it was not unusual to see Grey Wolf or a roaming Grizzly.

A mile further on from the lake, was a large beaver pond. It was stream fed by cool, clear water which ran down from the snow-capped ridges that bordered the valley. It was surrounded by grass and wild flowers and at its outlet end, Beavers had built a sturdy dam from the Lodge Pole pines and Aspen sited nearby.

It was here that a log cabin sat. This was Laramie's destination.

The three of them had only travelled a further thirty yards along the feint trail, when they were stopped by Laramie again. He listened for a moment then called, 'Get off the trail, quick!'

The trio immediately guided their horses off the trail and into a thick stand of Pine. Laramie and Slate dismounted then worked to keep the horses quiet. Soon after, Sally heard the reason for the group's hasty retreat into cover.

At first there came a low rumble which grew steadily louder. Around a blind bend, appeared maybe fifteen Blackfoot warriors as they thundered down the trail, bent low over their mounts to urge them on faster.

From where he sat, Laramie could see the war paint daubed on their faces. He frowned. This was the first he knew of trouble with the Blackfeet. Things had been peaceful for a long while.

The Indians disappeared down the trail and the drum of hooves gradually receded until the noise was gone.

'Looks like we weren't the only ones to hear all that gunfire,' Slate observed.

'Looks like,' agreed the gunfighter. 'But what I don't understand, is why those braves were painted for war.'

'I noticed that too,' said Slate.

'But there has been no trouble with them for a long time, so why now? What made them put on paint now?' Laramie wondered aloud.

'Who knows,' shrugged Slate, but the expression on his face clearly showed that he had more knowledge of the situation than he let on.

Laramie was suspicious but refused to say anything now. There would be time enough for that later. They needed to put distance between them and whatever it was that had the Blackfeet so riled. He climbed back into the saddle and gave Bo a slight touch with his heels and the Horse walked out of the trees. 'Come on then, let's go. But keep an eye out for any more Indians. The last thing we need is them on our trail.'

6

The posse was strung out along the rough trail when the light breeze brought the sound of the distant gun fire. Jeb Coltrain brought them all to a halt by a raised hand. His brother Zeb, rode up beside him and asked frustrated, 'Why are we stopping?'

Jeb looked at him and for a moment wondered if his brother was losing it. He shook his head and said evenly, 'I can hear gunfire up ahead.'

'Yes, so,' the judge dismissed it. 'I can hear it too. Hence my question, why are we stopping?'

'Well shoot, Judge, I ain't about to ride headlong into a gunfight I know nothin' about,' the Sheriff whipped around in the saddle. 'Jim, go and look.'

'Will do,' Jim Clancy said as he moved his mount forward past the Coltrain brothers.

'And stay out of sight,' the Sheriff added unnecessarily.

'We're wasting time sitting here Jeb,' said the judge.

'If it keeps us alive, then it isn't a waste of time, Judge.'

'And meanwhile that murdering son of a bitch is getting further away,' spat Zeb in frustration.

The Sheriff let it go. He could understand his brother's angst, but he needed to be a little more patient. They would catch Davis eventually, and then the judge could unleash his vengeance upon the gunfighter.

Fifteen minutes later, Jim Clancy returned at a gallop then dragged back on the reins and brought his Bay round and skidded to a halt.

'The way station is under attack from Indians, Jeb,' Clancy said concernedly.

'How many Indians are you talkin' about Jim?' asked Sheriff Coltrain, unperturbed.

'They look like they've been whittled down some, but my guess would be fifteen, maybe a few more.'

Jeb Coltrain thought for a moment, then drew his Colt and checked the loads. 'Alright,' he said loud enough for everyone to hear. 'Let's go kill us some redskins.'

'Now just hold on a minute Sheriff,' Orson Blake protested.

The Sheriff gave Blake a withering look. 'Do you have somethin' to say Blake?'

Orson thought about it briefly, then dropped his gaze and shook his head.

'Didn't think so,' Jeb focused his gaze on the judge. 'Reckon you can keep up on that mule of yours?'

The judge pulled the Webley revolver from his pocket. 'My mule could outrun that damn nag of yours on his worst day.'

'Alright then, let's go.'

*   *   *

'Hey Blackie, I'm getting' low on ammunition,' Benny shouted across to

79

the outlaw as the latest attack died away.

'You ain't the only one kid,' Harbin agreed. 'Another rush like that last one and I'll be all out.'

Things were bad. Since the initial assault, targets were hard to acquire. The Blackfeet would move in quickly and loose shots, then fall back. This caused the defenders to waste valuable ammunition even if they made the occasional kill shot.

'Keep an eye out,' Harbin said and ducked off to check the others.

Both had the same issues; too many Indians and not enough ammunition. Blackie called the group together. 'Listen up, you know how bad it is so this is what I propose to do. On the next attack, we go out that door and take the fight to them. Have all your weapons fully loaded and ready to go.'

'Not much of a plan,' Cato pointed out.

'Would you rather stay in here until we run out of ammunition?' Harbin asked scornfully.

'Didn't say that Blackie, just said it wasn't much of a plan,' Cato said defensively. 'But I guess it's better than the alternative.'

'Exactly,' Harbin agreed. 'Anybody else have an idea?'

Benny said, 'I always figured I'd go down in front of a gun. Just didn't think it would be a damn Redskin on the other end of it.'

'Perhaps you would like me to shoot you?' Lone Wolf asked, a smile on his face.

'Damn,' said Cato who shook his head in bewilderment. 'Now you smile. You who've never smiled in your life, pick when we are about to die, to start.'

A short while later, the Blackfeet came again, but this time the Harbin gang came out to meet them.

With Blackie in the lead, the gang emerged from the way station, all guns fired as fast as they could. The Indians were taken aback at such a foolhardy move and hesitated, which gave the outlaws a short-lived reprieve.

The Blackfeet increased their rate of fire but still the gang's luck held. Bullets kicked dirt up, like mini eruptions at their feet while others whizzed past, close enough for them to feel the displaced air. An arrow opened a thin cut on Lone Wolf's thigh while another gouged flesh from Cato's rib cage.

Things changed rapidly when Blackie Harbin went down.

★　★　★

The Posse came off the trail at full gallop, men yelled at the top of their voices while they fired their guns at the Indian Braves. Warriors scattered as the posse men cut a path between them and the outlaws. The increased amount of fire, set the Blackfeet back on their heels. In the first pass, the posse put down four Indians and as they turned to come back, the attack broke and the warriors scattered.

The posse men, however, didn't escape unscathed. When they turned to ride back through the yard, a lucky shot took Grover Yates in the chest and caused his bright red blood to spray across Orson Blake, then he slowly slid from the saddle, dead before he hit the earth.

Jim Clancy was wounded as well. An arrow burrowed into the fleshy part of his thigh, but unable to do anything about it, the unwanted intrusion remained in place for the time being.

Sheriff Jeb Coltrain sighted down the barrel of his Colt and fired a shot at the back of a retreating warrior. The gun bucked in his hand and he smiled as the bullet smashed into the Brave's head, spraying crimson. The Indian flopped to the ground, a lifeless heap amidst the carnage of battle. A shrill, almost human scream filled the air. Coltrain turned to look and saw the judge's mule go down, which threw the heavy man to the hard-packed yard. He tried to rise but the dead animal had him pinned by the leg.

The sheriff came out of his saddle

and rushed to his brother's side. 'Are you okay Zeb?'

'Help me out,' the judge bleated. 'The damn mule has my leg pinned.'

Jeb Coltrain holstered his gun, bent down and took his brother under the arms and heaved with all his strength. The judge slid out and Jeb let him flop on the ground.

The sheriff drew his gun again and looked around the swing station yard. The gunfire had ceased and the Indians were gone. Men started to get together to make sure they were all fine.

A dry triple click of a gun hammer caused the Sheriff to turn slowly, and he came face to face with Blackie Harbin.

'Nice of you to turn up law dog,' Blackie said through gritted teeth. 'Now how about you toss that gun of yours.'

Jeb noticed that Harbin had taken a shot to the left shoulder. Blood ran down his arm and dripped from the tips of his fingers. His face was a mask of pain and he was unsteady on his feet, but the six-gun he held in his right fist was rock steady.

The sheriff lowered his gun. 'Now hold on there stranger. You'd best think about it before you go and pull that trigger.'

'I said, lose the gun,' Harbin repeated the order.

Coltrain looked around the yard and noticed that posse men and outlaws alike, still had their weapons drawn but had them pointed at each other.

'What's your name?' he asked Harbin.

Harbin looked at him as if he were stupid. 'Don't you know? Hell Sheriff, I'm the notorious Blackie Harbin.'

The sheriff nodded. 'I heard of you. Mean son of a bitch, and low down murderer.'

Harbin smiled through the pain. 'You heard right.'

'I tell you what Harbin. How about we forget our paths ever crossed? Would that suit you?'

Harbin looked at the law man suspiciously. 'Now why would you do that?'

'Because it ain't you we're chasin',' Jeb explained. 'We are after the scum that killed my brother's boy, who also happened to be my deputy. Feller by the name of Laramie Davis.'

Harbin laughed bitterly.

'What's funny?' the sheriff asked, curious.

'Hell, Laramie was here last night Sheriff,' Harbin explained, his voice full of mirth. 'Matter of fact he left sometime during the night and took somethin' of mine with him.'

'Where did he go?' the judge burst out eagerly. 'Answer me man, I must know so the killer can hang.'

'Ease up Judge,' Jeb cautioned his brother.

'Well, well, a judge too. This just gets better.' Harbin went quiet, trying to think.

'Are we goin' to shoot 'em Blackie?' Benny asked his boss from halfway across the yard.

'Shut up a moment kid, I'm busy.'

Harbin looked thoughtfully at the

Sheriff. 'I tell you what law man, since you and I are goin' to be after the same man, how about we join up together and do it that way.'

There were two reasons for Harbin's suggestion. The first was the Indians. He knew, without a doubt, that they would be back. The second was the ammunition situation, as he had no bullets left in his gun. He couldn't shoot the Sheriff even if he'd wanted to.

'No!' barked the judge.

Jeb ignored his brother. 'Alright we'll do it that way, but I don't want no grief. Any trouble from your boys and they'll have me to deal with. That goes for you too.'

Harbin's eyes glittered and he broke into a churlish grin as he lowered his gun. 'Looks like we got ourselves a deal.'

'Fine then,' affirmed Jeb Coltrain. 'We'd best see to the dead and wounded.'

★　★　★

The trio topped Frenchie's Pass early in the afternoon and the vista before them, was one of the most beautiful sights that Sally had ever seen. The lush, green meadows, the giant trees from an ageless time, and the sun's reflection on the crystal-clear water of the lake that sparkled like diamonds. The effect was breathtakingly spectacular.

'That is amazing,' she marvelled softly, as she tried to find her voice. 'I never knew a place like this existed. It's unbelievable.'

'As old Lonesome says, it's about as close to heaven as a man can get, without dyin'.'

'I think I tend to agree with him, whoever he is,' Sally said, her mouth agape in awe, 'What's it called? This valley, what's its name?'

Laramie shook his head. 'Beaver Valley.'

'Who's Old Lonesome?' Slate asked.

'He's an old trapper, goes by the name of Lonesome Lane,' explained

Laramie. 'He's been livin' in this valley since forever. You'll meet him later, as we should reach his cabin before dark.'

The trail down into the valley was narrow. It twisted through tall Ponderosa, and turned past large, jagged rock formations. At one point, the path tapered down to a constricted ledge that ran along a sheer cliff face with a drop of over five hundred feet, before it opened up again and curved away through another stand of trees. Occasionally, a small rivulet of water cut the rider's path and continued its course to the drop off, where it formed one of many scattered, miniature waterfalls.

On their arrival at the base of the valley, the trail came out into a broad meadow and the trio found themselves riding through grass, thick and tall enough to touch their horse's flanks.

For the rest of the afternoon they followed the trail as it meandered across small, swift flowing streams that bubbled and gurgled over their rocky bottoms, dappled sunlight creating a hypnotic effect. On the north shore of the small lake, the riders startled some elk that grazed upon an abundance of sweet grass. The horses picked their way along the bank of a slow stream and headed toward a large dam built and maintained by a small beaver population which inhabited the deep pond formed by the wall.

Beyond the beaver pond, and its furry residents, lay their destination. A rough-hewn log cabin with wooden shutters and smoke that curled lazily from a stone chimney. The home of Lonesome Lane.

As they approached the cabin, a man stepped through the doorway and levelled an ancient Hawken rifle in Laramie's direction. 'Hold it right there, Pilgrim, I'd hate to paint that there fancy horse of yours a nice shade of red.'

★ ★ ★

While Laramie stared into the gaping muzzle of Lonesome's Hawken, the posse, boosted by the remains of Blackie Harbin's gang, approached a flat strip of land, sparsely covered by trees, just shy of Frenchie's Pass.

'We'll camp here for the night,' ordered Jeb Coltrain. He pointed at a fast-flowing stream which split the bench. 'Plenty of water and flat ground.'

It suited Harbin. His shoulder wound throbbed something fierce, and he wanted a chance to clean it again.

'What about the Indians?' the judge asked, concerned. 'Won't they come back?'

'That was my thinkin' too,' whined Orson Blake. 'We should have turned back after they high tailed it.'

Blake had felt that way since they'd buried Grover Yates in his unmarked grave. Not the only one to voice his opinion, both Blake and Clay Adams, the young cow hand, had had their say. The pair and their misgivings, were overridden by the Coltrains.

'Shut up Blake, your whinin' is

startin' to annoy me,' Jeb Coltrain said forcefully before he answered his brother's question, 'It's possible, but I think with the lickin' they received today, maybe they'll go and tend their wounds for a while.'

The judge seemed mollified by that.

With the horses unsaddled and picketed, the sheriff walked across to Blackie Harbin. 'One of yours and one of mine on first watch. Do you have a problem with that?'

'Nope, no problem at all law man.'

Behind them, a disturbance near the horses grabbed their attention and they turned to see Shell and Benny faced off, their hands hovered over their gun butts.

'What did you say?' Benny hissed.

'I said you're a damn wannabe,' Shell spat.

'We'll see about that. What say we find out how good I really am?' bragged Benny.

'You call it, Tin horn,' came Shell's insult.

'Hold it!'

The words that erupted from Sheriff Jeb Coltrain's lips, stayed both hands. 'There'll be no gun play. Here or anywhere else for that matter.'

Benny started to speak, 'He damn well . . . '

'Benny, shut up!' Blackie Harbin bellowed. 'Go and take first watch.'

'But . . . '

'Just do it!'

Benny glared at Shell Coltrain then turned quickly and stalked off, the mumble under his breath almost inaudible.

'You too, Shell,' said the Sheriff.

The deputy opened his mouth to protest.

'Get gone,' his uncle said as he flung his arm into the air and overrode him.

Blackie watched Shell go and said, 'I have a feelin' things are goin' to be mighty interestin' around here Law dog.'

'Ain't that the truth,' Jeb agreed. 'Just remember, I didn't pass out most of our spare ammunition just for you and yours to shoot us with.'

* * *

'Hold your fire you damned old ridge runner,' Laramie said and held up his hands. 'Are you blind or somethin'?'

'Hell, I know that voice,' Lonesome Lane said, surprised. 'Laramie, is that you boy?'

'Yeah Lonesome, it's me,' the gunfighter confirmed.

'Well shoot boy,' beamed Lonesome as he lowered the Hawken, 'get your butt off that damn mule of yours and over here where I can see you proper.'

'What about my friends?'

The ageing trapper nodded. 'Sure, them too.'

Laramie and the others dismounted and walked over to where the old man stood. It had been a good while since Laramie had paid Lonesome a visit, the change evident in the colour of the Mountain man's beard which now matched the snow white of his hair. His face held the ravages of time, the many contours of age, and his wide shoulders looked as though they carried the weight of the world.

'Damn boy, what brings you all the way up here?'

Laramie expelled a large breath and said seriously, 'I have myself a slight problem.'

7

'A slight problem you say?' Lonesome shook his head. 'Son, I'd say that just maybe it's a little bit of an understatement, wouldn't you.'

'Maybe,' Laramie conceded.

The gunfighter had filled Lonesome in on his ordeal after Sally and Slate had been introduced to the old trapper.

'Stay as long as you like, son,' Lonesome invited. 'I haven't had a good scrap in an age. Some excitement around here would be good.'

Laramie shook his head. 'We'll just stay the night if it's all the same, don't want you getting' caught up in our troubles.'

'Suit yourself son, anyway come on inside. I reckon the young lady could use a seat that ain't movin' around of its own accord.'

Sally smiled warmly. 'You reckon

right, Mister Lane.'

Lonesome raised his eyebrows. 'And she's respectful. Come on Missy, it's been a long time since I talked to a lovely lass such as yourself. I'm goin' to enjoy havin' you around even if it is only for one night.'

The old man turned to step inside when Laramie asked, 'Hey Lonesome, do you know anythin' about the Blackfeet kickin' up a stink.'

'First, I've heard of it,' said the trapper, who continued to walk into the cabin.

*   *   *

Far off up the valley, a wolf's howl was answered by the high-pitched shriek of a mountain lion. The moon was up and the clear mountain air held a slight chill. Laramie and Slate sat in front of the cabin on the rickety porch, where they discussed Blackie Harbin's plans

'Where was Blackie headin' after you hit the stage?' he asked the outlaw.

'He's got a hideout over near Eagle Falls. Do you know where that is?'

Laramie nodded, 'Yeah, about a day's ride from Mountain Pass, where we're headin'.'

'That's right. There is an old abandoned minin' shack there. Blackie's been usin' it for two years or so, and no one ever goes near the place.'

'I find it strange that the law ain't found it,' Laramie wondered out loud.

'It's not that easy to find,' Slate explained. 'There's a box canyon to the north of Eagle Falls with a narrow mouth, and the cabin's set way back in a stand of trees. Unless you know where to look, or stumble upon it, you wouldn't know it's there.'

A noise behind them drew their attention. Sally Richards had emerged from the cabin unnoticed.

'He's gone to sleep,' she explained.

Slate stood up from where he was seated and brushed himself off. 'I'll just go check the horses.'

After he was gone, Sally said, 'I

didn't mean to chase him away.'

Laramie shrugged it off. 'Don't let it worry you.'

Sally looked up at the broad expanse of the star filled sky and sighed heavily, 'It's beautiful here Laramie. I can see why Mister Lane would choose to live here.'

'It's certainly a special place,' he agreed. 'As long as I've known him, he's never wanted to be anywhere else.'

'Oh, how long have you known him?'

'I was quite a young man when I first met Lonesome. It was shortly after I'd joined the Marshal's and I was on a job trackin' down a wanted man,' Laramie smiled, 'and I got lost.'

'Really?'

'Oh yeah, hopelessly lost. Anyway, I happened to hear some shootin' goin' on and ridin' to the sound of the guns, I came across Lonesome havin' a good set to with some natives. Well bein' a young buck and showin' no fear, I rode straight into that fight and got shot.'

Sally tried to cover her smile. 'Oh, no.'

'Yes, lookin' back now, it does seem funny,' he allowed. 'But at the time, it hurt somethin' fierce. When I came to, Lonesome had patched me up and then brought me back here to mend. It was quite ironic, here was me, I tried to save his life and instead it ended up, he saved mine. We've been friends ever since. Helped me out of a scrape a time or two as well.'

Sally thought for a moment. 'How old is he?'

The gunfighter smiled at her. 'Don't rightly know myself, but if I had to guess I'd say he's seen a lot of seasons and leave it at that. I do know one thing though, don't let his age fool you. Under that crusty old exterior is one tough man, he's had to be to survive this long.'

Sally changed the subject. 'When will we reach Mountain Pass?'

'Providin' it all goes to plan, you'll be home in two days,' Laramie answered. 'That's if we don't have any troubles.'

'Why did you stop?' Sally asked

bluntly. 'I mean, back at the way station, you could have kept riding and forgotten all about it, not become involved.'

'I guess that's the Marshal in me,' he explained truthfully. 'I couldn't keep ridin'. My conscience wouldn't let me. It's a flaw that I have. Even when I sell my gun, it's always for the right cause.'

'Can I ask you a personal question?'

'Sure, why not?' he answered, curious.

'If you feel that way, why leave the Marshal Service? Surely it was better to be a Marshal than a gunman?'

For a moment, Laramie couldn't speak. No person had asked him that question before.

'I'm sorry,' Sally apologised. 'Please, it really is none of my business so don't answer if you don't want to.'

'No, it's fine,' Laramie replied and tried to ease her embarrassment. 'What it boils down to, is the choice wasn't mine. The Marshal's let me go.'

Sally was confused. 'But why? If you

were so good at your job, what possible reason could they have to let you go?'

Laramie told her the story. 'All my life I've been good with a gun, so when I joined the Marshal's they would give me special assignments. The tough nuts to crack, so to speak. The main job that came my way was to bring law and order to wild towns. Pretty soon I became known as the Marshal's specialist Town Tamer.'

He paused before he continued, 'The more towns I tamed, the bigger my reputation became and before long, I was looked upon as a hired gun more than a United States Marshal. Shortly after that, the Marshal's decided it was a reputation they didn't want associated with the law, so they let me go.'

'I'm sorry,' Sally said quietly.

'Don't be, lookin' back now, they were probably right.'

There was an uneasy silence for a few moments before Laramie said, 'You'd best turn in. We have us a long ride comin' up tomorrow.'

'Yes, you're right,' Sally agreed as she stood up. 'Goodnight Laramie.'

'Goodnight Sally.'

★　★　★

Shortly after dawn, three steaming plates of food sat in front of the men. Laramie looked at the brown, gluey substance and then questioningly at Sally.

'What is it?' he asked cautiously.

'You don't want to know,' she blanched in disgust.

He looked across the table at Lonesome who shovelled great forkfuls of whatever it was, into his mouth. Slate on the other hand, ate tentatively, like a bird would peck at seeds on the ground.

Laramie looked once more at Sally who shook her head slightly to discourage him from the pile on his plate. He frowned, aware that something was wrong, and it wasn't until Lonesome spoke, that he found out what it was.

'Missy,' the old Trapper garbled, his

mouth half full of food, 'this just has to be the best skunk stew I've eaten since Fifty-Eight.'

Laramie screwed up his face and pushed the old tin plate away. He glanced across at Slate who had turned a slight shade of green and excused himself quickly as he expelled the contents of his mouth.

The gunfighter looked at Sally. 'Where's yours?'

Her expression stoic, she said, 'Thanks, but I've already eaten.'

Laramie was about to say more when a noise from outside drew his attention. He rose from his chair, crossed to a window, and drew one of his Remingtons as he went. He eased back the flap of hide which passed for a curtain. It parted enough for him to see five Blackfoot warriors ease their ponies to a stop outside the cabin. All of them, their horses included, were painted for war.

The cabin door opened and Laramie turned to see Lonesome disappear out it and onto the porch. Then he realised that the old man was unarmed. He thumbed back the hammer of his gun and waited.

'What's happening?' asked Sally, a slight quiver in her voice after having seen the gunfighter cock his weapon.

He held up his hand to quiet her.

With the use of words and hand gestures, the Indians and the old Trapper communicated for five minutes. At one stage of the conversation, one of the Braves pointed to the cabin. With a furious head shake by Lonesome, the Indians seemed convinced of what the mountain man told them.

With the confrontation over, the warriors backed their paint daubed ponies away from where Lonesome stood and rode off. The old man watched them go before he turned and went back inside.

Once he was back indoors, Laramie eased the hammer down on his gun and holstered it.

'What did they want?' asked Laramie curiously.

'It seems,' Lonesome started before

he turned his angry gaze upon Slate, 'that someone killed their chief's brother. And his brother's wife.'

Laramie's gaze shifted to Slate. 'What else did they say?'

'They said there were six of them that done it. Killed the warrior and done bad things to the woman. Their names were Lame Bear and Lost Dove. The braves are on their way to join up with Black Elk,' Lonesome paused. 'Now considering the circumstances that bring you here, I got to wonder if this feller here is involved somehow.'

Laramie nodded. 'I'm thinkin' the same thing. How about it Slate? Were you involved?'

Slate's eyes grew wide. 'No, not me! I didn't do anythin' Laramie, I swear!'

'But you were there,' it was a statement, not a question.

Slate's shoulders fell and he looked at the floor like a child being lectured for doing something wrong.

'Yeah, I was there,' he conceded before he lifted his gaze to look the gunfighter in the eye. 'But I didn't do anythin' wrong.

Laramie shook his head sorrowfully. 'Hell Slate, just bein' there was wrong.'

The outlaw nodded silently.

'So, what happened?'

Slate heaved a sigh, a look of pain crossed his face as he began to relate the events. 'We came upon them when we was headin' to Four Trails. They seemed friendly enough, a little wary, but we didn't give 'em any cause to fear us. I thought we was goin' to ride right on past 'em, but when we was level with 'em, Blackie just pulled his gun and shot the Indian Brave point blank.'

Slate paused, his expression now crestfallen. 'Then there was the woman. Hell, I ain't never seen anythin' like that before, what they did to her. I close my eyes and I can still see it.'

'Who did it?' asked Laramie.

'It was Blackie and the kid, Benny,' the outlaw answered. 'I tried to stop 'em Laramie, honest I did, but Blackie told Cato to hold a gun on me until they were finished.'

Lonesome snatched up his Hawken. 'I oughta put a lead ball in you right now, you blasted . . . '

Sally gasped as Slate leaped back when the old man swung the Hawken around and pulled back the hammer.

'Hold it Lonesome!' Laramie cried.

The mountain man had moved so quickly that it surprised them all, and now he had the rifle pointed at Slate's head with his finger curled on the trigger. 'Why in hell should I?'

'Well, the way I see it, he has two choices.'

'What choices?' Lonesome's aim never wavered.

'We can cut him loose right now and he can take his chances with the Black-feet,' Laramie explained, 'or he can come back to Mountain Pass, talk to the law there and take what they give him.'

'Not much of a damn choice,' Slate sneered.

'Damn it boy, let me shoot the varmint,' Lonesome snarled.

The outlaw held both hands out in front. 'No, wait! Wait! I'll go back. I'll talk to the law, just don't let that crazy old coot kill me.'

Laramie nodded. 'Okay then, go and get the horses ready to leave. We should have been gone ages ago.'

'And don't get no idea's about runnin' either sonny. I may be old but I can still shoot straight.'

Slate said nothing as he walked out the door.

'You should've let me shoot him boy,' Lonesome opined.

'Do you think he will go through with it?' Sally questioned.

'I guess we'll find out.'

A while later the horses were saddled and all three were ready to depart. 'Are you sure you don't want to come with us? You know they'll be comin' this way.'

Lonesome gave a raspy chuckle. 'Son, I've fought Indians and faced down grizz. You don't think a bunch of pesky old outlaws is goin' to scare me any do ya? Besides, this is my home and this is where I plan on dyin'.'

Laramie held out his hand and Lonesome took it in his firm, rough grasp. 'I'll see you when the snow flies.'

'You damn well better,' the old man said gruffly.

'When they come, tell them which way we went. Don't get mixed up in it as it's not your fight.'

'Don't you worry about me.'

They turned their horses and rode away, and left the old trapper where he stood and watched them as they went.

'Do you think he will be alright?' Sally asked, a hint of sadness in her voice.

'I hope so Sally, I sure hope so.'

* * *

There were ten of them altogether but only nine were lined up in front of Lonesome Lane. The other, a Crow Indian walked a wide path, and looked for sign. Since Laramie and the others had gone, the old mountain man had sat and waited for the pursuers to come. Now he faced them with the Hawken pointed in their direction, its hammer on full cock.

'Are you blind old man?' asked Jeb Coltrain in frustration. 'Can't you see this badge? It says Sheriff.'

Lonesome smiled coldly. 'It's right purty. Now, have you ever seen what a lead ball can do to one of them nice shiny badges you're wearin'?'

The Sheriff was out of patience. 'I asked you a question. Were they here and where did they go?'

'No, they weren't here and I don't know where they went and that was two questions.'

Benny moved his horse forward, 'Damn you old man . . . '

The Hawken moved and its gaping muzzle settled on the kid. 'Now sonny, just you pull them horns of yours in before I go and teach you some manners.'

'Back off kid, let the sheriff handle it,' said Harbin.

'He ain't goin' to tell us squat Blackie,' Benny whined.

Lonesome redirected his gaze until it rested on the boss outlaw. 'So you're the great Blackie Harbin. You and yours are the ones the Blackfeet is lookin' for.'

Blackie's eyes hardened.

'Did he tell you what he did Sheriff?'

'Shut up old man,' Harbin grated.

'He killed himself an Indian. Not just any Indian, the brother of a chief no less.'

Harbin pulled the flap of his duster aside, and exposed one of his pearl handled Colts. 'I told you to shut up, I won't tell you again.'

The old trapper ignored the killer's threats and continued, 'But it didn't stop there. He had himself a great time with the braves' wife before he cut her throat!'

'Damn you,' Harbin cursed and his hand blurred. The Colt cleared leather and before the old man could bring the Hawken into line, a single shot crashed out. The .45 calibre slug caught

Lonesome in the chest, and knocked him back. As he went down, the mountain man lost grip of his prized possession and it fell into the grass beside him. As Laramie had told Sally, Lonesome was tough, and the old timer struggled back up to his knees. He looked Harbin in the eye and tried to speak. No words came forth and after a few hard-fought seconds of trying to stay erect, Lonesome Lane fell face first into the grass and remained still.

'No, what have you done!' cried the judge.

'What in hell did you go and do that for Harbin?' cursed the Sheriff.

'He talked too much,' shrugged Harbin.

'Is what he said true?' questioned the Sheriff.

'And what if it is?' the outlaw challenged.

'It damn well explains a lot.'

Before more could be said, Lone Wolf returned. 'I found their trail leadin' away from here.'

'Which way are they headin'?' the Sheriff asked.

Lone Wolf pointed up the valley. 'There is more. This mornin', Indians were here. Five of them.'

'Who cares about them,' Harbin brushed the cautionary warning away. 'It's them others we are after. How far ahead are they?'

'Maybe three hours.'

'Let's get going then,' said the judge as he fought to get his horse turned. 'Damned animal of Grover's is as stubborn as that old goat was.'

'Okay then,' said Jeb Coltrain, 'you lead out Indian.'

The group swung their horses away from Lonesome's cabin and followed Lone Wolf as he led them away from the solitary figure that lay face down on the ground.

8

Laramie called a halt around noon so they could water their horses at a rocky stream which cut a path through a small meadow. The water was clear and cool, and while the horses drank their fill, the gunfighter topped up the canteens.

'Look, over there,' said Sally, as she pointed to something in the meadow.

Laramie looked and saw a large bull elk, that had just stepped out of a stand of spruce, his antler rack magnificent. He stood quietly for a moment then stretched out his neck and emitted a high pitched, bugling call.

Sally was awe struck. 'What a wonderful animal.'

Laramie agreed. 'He's just lettin' us know we're in his territory.'

Sally watched as the Elk remained still for a while longer before he turned and disappeared into the trees.

'Laramie, come and have a look at this,' Slate called from where he watered his horse a little farther upstream.

He left Bo to drink and walked across to Slate. 'What is it?'

Slate pointed to a patch of damp dirt beside the stream. 'Look there.'

In the middle of a bare spot was a solitary, unshod hoof print. The sight of it caused a chill to run up Laramie's back. He lifted his eyes and scanned his surroundings, then he looked back at the source of his worry. 'Couldn't be more than a couple of hours old.'

'That's what I was thinkin',' Slate agreed.

Laramie looked about some more. 'I'll be happier when we can get out of the open. The trail cuts through the trees up ahead. I'll feel better then, let's go.'

They mounted up and said nothing of their discovery to Sally.

Once the path entered the trees,

Laramie breathed a sigh of relief. He'd watched their back trail but could detect no one following, but that only meant that nobody was visible. The trail weaved its way through tall pine trees, their aromatic scent hung heavily in the air. The gunfighter let the big Appaloosa pick his way along an undulating path that dropped into a gully. He crossed another of the many streams and climbed the slope on the other side.

The trail started to rise steadily and over the course of a few hours, the ground became rockier, and large, grey outcrops became more frequent. The forest thinned out substantially once the path topped the ridge line and continued along its spine.

Laramie eased Bo to a halt. 'We'll rest here for the moment.'

Where they sat, the riders had a clear view into the next valley. It was not much different from the one they had just ridden out of, except there were more trees and no lake. A river meandered across the valley floor, and bisected the wilderness in its path.

Sally pulled her horse up beside Laramie's. 'This country just keeps going. It's magnificent.'

'Do you see where the river bends around that rock formation, on the other side of those trees?'

Sally looked to where he pointed. 'Yes, I think so.'

'We'll camp there tonight and we should reach Mountain Pass late tomorrow afternoon.'

Sally nodded. 'I will be happy to get back.'

* * *

Laramie poked the small fire with a stick and caused it to flare, sending off little sparks that danced in the night air before it died down again. In the surrounding darkness, the croak of frogs was loudly accentuated by the stillness of the night. Somewhere close, a wolf's howl made the horses stir and fidget nervously. Slate stood and walked over to the animals to soothe them.

Laramie stood and crossed the camp site to talk to Slate while Sally enjoyed the small amount of warmth provided by the fire. After their conversation, Slate picked up his rifle from beside his saddle and walked out into the night.

'Where is he going?' Sally asked curiously.

'He's goin' to take watch,' Laramie explained. 'Just in case we get any unwanted visitors.'

'Do we need to put the fire out?'

The gunfighter shook his head. 'No, it should be alright. That was why we set up in these rocks, it'll kill the glow of the fire some.'

Sally shivered. 'I was hoping you would say that, it's getting cold.'

'If you turn in next to the fire and keep your blanket wrapped around you, you should be fine,' Laramie explained.

'I hope you're right.'

An hour later, with Slate still on watch, Sally and Laramie rolled up in their blankets and went to sleep on opposite sides of the fire. The plan was, that in a few hours, Slate would wake Laramie, who would take over watch. Like a lot of plans formulated throughout history, this one didn't work out.

★　★　★

At first Laramie couldn't work out what had roused him. The fire had burned low, but he wasn't cold. Sally was asleep and peaceful, so that wasn't it. There was a slight breeze in the trees which made a low whistling sound. Apart from that, it was relatively quiet. Even the . . .

He stopped and listened. The frogs, yes, the frogs were too quiet. Something had caused them to cease their song. They should still be croaking, unless . . .

Laramie eased his hand out and wrapped it around the butt of one of his Remingtons. He slid it slowly out of its holster. There came the triple click of a gun hammer being eared back to full cock. It wasn't his.

'Just put the gun down Davis, nice and easy,' came a low, familiar voice.

Laramie cursed under his breath and put the pistol down.

'Now stand up, real slow.'

He did as ordered, and once up, was face to face with the Sheriff of Rock Springs.

There was a scream from Sally as Blackie Harbin dragged her roughly by the hair and forced her to her feet. Laramie made to move to her aid but was stopped short when the sheriff's six-gun dug into his ribs.

Jeb Coltrain smiled wickedly. 'I have someone with me who's been dyin' to meet you.'

The sheriff nodded and there was a swift movement from behind. Something hard smashed into the back of the gunfighter's head and caused him to sink to his knees. His ears rang and through it all he heard Sally scream again.

Laramie shook his head to clear the cobwebs and struggled to his feet. A little shaken, he turned to faced his attacker.

The man was short and very rotund and his right hand held a large tree branch. So that's what hit me, Laramie thought, then became aware of the small trickle of blood on the back of his neck.

'You damned murderer,' cursed the judge. 'You killed my boy.'

He raised the branch to strike again, but Laramie's survival skills kicked in before the judge could start his down-swing.

The gunfighter's head snapped forward and caught the judge across the bridge of his nose. Cartilage crunched and blood spurted as Zebulon Coltrain emitted a howl of pain, staggered backwards and clutched at his ruined nose.

Jeb Coltrain grabbed Laramie roughly about the throat and pressed his Colt hard to the side of his head. 'Do some-thin' like that again and we'll just hang you right here,' he warned.

'Son of a bitch,' the judge cried out.

'He broke my nose!'

He pulled his hand away from his face to find it covered in blood, 'I'm going to enjoy hanging you,' he spat a great glob of blood onto the ground. 'Damn you.'

There was more commotion as Slate was pushed into the camp by Benny and Cato. He looked at Laramie, fear etched deep into his face. 'I'm sorry Laramie,' he apologised. 'I fell asleep. I'm so sorry.'

'Don't worry about it, kid,' he said softly. 'It could've happened to anyone.'

Harbin pushed Sally aside and walked purposefully over to Slate, who knew what was about to happen.

'Well, well. If it isn't the double-crosser. Do you remember when you joined our little band, what it was that I said about double-crossers? And do you remember what I said would happen if you ever double-crossed me?'

Slate remained silent.

'Do you?' Harbin snapped.

Benny and Cato stepped away as

Slate nodded weakly.

'Leave him be Harbin!' Laramie snapped.

Blackie Harbin gave Laramie a look of pure evil and said, 'He was warned.'

Harbin swiftly drew one of his pearl handled Colts and shot Slate in the head. It snapped back savagely as the .45 calibre slug blew blood and gore out the back when it exited.

Laramie squeezed his eyes shut as rage built up inside of him. He tried to block out the laugh of Benny and the cry of anguish that escaped from Sally. He drew in a couple of deep breaths and opened his eyes.

'I'm goin' to kill you for that Harbin,' Laramie said coldly. 'Just you wait and see. It may not be tonight, but it will happen. Count on it.'

'You seem to forget, Davis,' Jeb Coltrain hissed in his ear. 'I have a prior claim. On you.'

He shoved Laramie forward and the gunfighter staggered a little before he regained his balance.

Laramie looked about in search of Sally. He saw her, on her knees, face in her hands, as she tried to deal with the cold-blooded manner of Slate's death. Her shoulders trembled as she sobbed silently, the sight of what Harbin had done, etched deep in her mind alongside that of the salesman from the stage.

Laramie stumbled a couple of steps toward her, but Shell blocked his path.

'Are you goin' somewhere killer?' the deputy asked with a wicked smile.

Laramie made to move around him, but Shell's fist travelled swiftly and the blow took him in the midriff. He doubled over as the air rushed from his lungs, and a hammer blow to the back of his head, took him to his hands and knees in a slump. Through the fog that clouded his mind, he heard Sally scream for it to stop.

A hand grabbed his shirt and dragged him to his feet. Through blurred vision, Laramie could just make out the face of Shell Coltrain, a smile plastered across it. He struck a vicious blow to Laramie's face and split his lips as they mashed against his teeth. A second blow snapped his head back and it bobbled about, senseless from the last blow. Blood flowed freely from a cut on his face and. things grew dark as consciousness began to leave him.

Shell let go of Laramie's shirt. The gunfighter collapsed to the ground with a low moan.

The judge stepped forward and lashed out with his boot, anger and frustration evident in his actions. It landed solidly and Laramie felt pain shoot through his ribs. The second blow followed by another, glanced off his shoulder before it collected him in the side of the head. Mercifully, darkness finally claimed him.

'Whoa, hold on there, judge,' the sheriff tried to calm his brother. 'Try to leave somethin' for the hangman.'

The old man blew hard from his exertions. 'Alive or dead he's still going to hang. You mark my words. He'll hang and everyone will see what we do to murderers who kill our own.'

'Tie him up Shell,' Jeb Coltrain ordered his nephew. 'We'll stay until mornin' and then head back to Rock Springs.'

Shell rolled Laramie's prone form over and bound the gunman's hands behind him with a strip of rawhide. He dragged the body over to where Sally sat and dropped him roughly to the ground. She immediately started to tend his wounds to make sure he was okay.

'May I have some water?' she asked Shell Coltrain. 'Just to clean him up a little.'

The younger Coltrain sneered, 'Hell no. Be happy with the fact he is still alive. It's more than he deserves and more than my brother got.'

He turned and walked away.

As she returned her attention back to Laramie, a canteen appeared in front of her eyes. Sally looked up as Orson Blake stood over her.

He smiled warmly. 'Here, take it.'

Sally took the canteen and asked hopefully, 'Can you help me?'

Blake shook his head sadly. 'No, I'm sorry. I should not have even given you that.'

He turned away without another word and walked off.

$$\star \quad \star \quad \star$$

'Cato,' Harbin called out, 'where in hell are you?'

The outlaw emerged from the dark as he buttoned his flies. 'I'm here, stop yellin'.'

Harbin pointed at Slate's cooling body. 'Get rid of that will you, before it starts stinkin' up the place. After that, keep an eye on the girl. When we ride in the mornin', she's comin' with us.'

Cato looked at Harbin, the look on his face said, you shot him, you get rid of him, but decided against voicing his opinion. Instead, he bent down, took the body by the hands and dragged

Slate unceremoniously out of camp.

Harbin looked around for Benny and found him going through Laramie's belongings.

'What in hell are you doin' kid?' Harbin asked curiously.

'Just lookin',' Benny said without an upward glance.

'Just remember, any money you find gets split,' Blackie warned him.

Benny straightened up, unhappy. 'What about his guns, can I have them?'

Harbin shrugged. 'Sure, why not.'

Benny unbuckled his scarred Peacemakers and strapped on Laramie's Remingtons. He tied the rawhide thongs about his thighs and fiddled with the gun belt until it felt comfortable.

He smiled at Harbin. 'There, now I'm a damned legend too.'

Harbin shook his head in bemusement. 'Takes more than a gun to make a man, kid.'

Benny's ugly stare burned holes in Blackie Harbin's back as he walked away.

★ ★ ★

Soon after sun up, the mountain air was cool and fresh with the scent of pine and wood smoke. The horses stamped their feet, eager to be on the trail. Laramie had spent a cold, uncomfortable night with his hands tied behind his back.

In the aftermath of his beating, everything hurt. His ribs were tender from the judge's kicks and his face bore the signs of Shell's attack. His lips were cut and tender, and one eye was bruised and swollen. The small cut above his temple had stopped bleeding, but the residual headache was testament to the judge's kick that had caught him in the side of his head.

Laramie rolled so he could face Sally, his muscles screamed with the effort and a low moan escaped his battered lips.

'How are you doin' Sally?' he whispered so his voice wouldn't carry.

'I'm scared,' she answered honestly.

'What will happen to me?'

Laramie tried to reassure her. 'Just do what they say and you'll be fine. Don't make any trouble or give them any excuse to hurt you. When I can get away from these men, I'll come after you.'

'But how? How are you going to get away? If you try, they'll kill you,' the tears welled in her large brown eyes.

'If I don't escape, they'll make me swing from a rope,' he said with a grim expression. 'So I don't have much choice.'

'There's something else,' Sally said tentatively.

Laramie waited for her to continue.

'I heard two of them talking last night while you were asleep. They were talking about . . . ,' Sally paused to gather herself, 'Blackie Harbin shot Lonesome. I'm so sorry Laramie, he shot him dead.'

The news hit him like a locomotive. The physical blows that he'd received the night before did not hurt the way this did. He felt an overwhelming sadness at the loss of his friend, quickly followed by a huge sense of guilt. If he hadn't gone there with the pursuers on his trail, the old man would still be alive.

Sally watched as Laramie's face changed. She could see it in his eyes first, as the anger started to take hold. His gaze became like ice and then his jaw set firm as he fought to contain his rage.

'Stay safe,' he said through gritted teeth. 'I'll come for you. You can count on that. And when I do, I'm goin' to kill that black hearted son of a bitch.'

When Cato came for Sally, she was reluctant to stand as he ordered her to. She looked to Laramie for help, the fear in her eyes evident. Laramie nodded to her and mouthed the words, 'I'm coming.'

It was a lot of faith to put in one man, virtually a stranger to her, who was at this point, a captive himself, but something in his eyes, perhaps a great determination, seemed to calm her. Sally stood and went with Cato to the horses, where he helped her up onto one of them.

Blackie Harbin approached and stood in front of Laramie. 'You know it's a shame it has to be this way Davis. Me personally, I would have liked to find out who was faster, but I guess we already know that anyway.'

Laramie said coolly, 'How about you untie me and we find out.'

Harbin shook his head. 'Noooo. That ain't goin' to happen. You see I promised the Sheriff, him and the judge could have you.'

'Scared Blackie?' Laramie challenged.

There was a small flash of anger in the outlaw's eyes as the barb hit a nerve, but Blackie, seemingly unperturbed, said 'No, can't say as I am.'

The conversation dried up for a moment before Harbin said, 'Well I guess this is goodbye then.'

'I'll be seein' you Blackie,' Laramie said with a hard edge to his voice.

Harbin looked at him quizzically and for a moment, the gunfighter thought there was a hint of fear in his eyes. It was a fleeting thing, and Harbin turned away and walked over to the horses.

Five minutes later Laramie watched the outlaws ride out, and Sally Richards with them.

*   *   *

'Okay killer, your turn,' said the sheriff of Rock Springs as he gave Laramie a nudge with his boot, 'stand up and get on over to your horse.'

Laramie struggled to his feet, his efforts caused fresh streaks of pain to shoot through his body. He shuffled over to where Bo was tethered, stood and waited.

'What is the problem?' asked the Sheriff.

'How do you expect me to get on my horse with my hands tied behind my back? Are you goin' to lift me?'

Jeb Coltrain mumbled in frustration. He walked behind Laramie and untied the rawhide from the gunfighter's wrists.

The burning sensation was instant as the circulation returned. Laramie winced as he tried to rub the pain away.

Jeb Coltrain grew impatient. 'Come on Davis, stop dawdlin'. Get on your horse and hurry it up.'

Once more, pain screamed through his side as he used the bruised muscles of his battered body. He threw his leg over and sat up straight in the saddle.

'Grab the saddle horn,' the sheriff ordered.

Laramie did as instructed; the rawhide was wrapped around and his hands were fastened to the pommel.

'Why did you let Harbin shoot the old man?' Laramie asked flatly.

The sheriff was about to walk away but paused and looked up at the gunfighter. 'I didn't let him shoot the old feller. I didn't even know he was goin' to do it until after the fact. Why? What was he to you?'

Laramie's eyes were emotionless. 'He was my friend.'

Coltrain shrugged apathetically. 'Well, your friend became an outlaw the moment he helped a wanted killer on the run from the law. I guess he got what was comin' to him.'

Laramie churned inside.

Coltrain waited for a reaction, but when one failed to emerge, he turned and walked away. He climbed into his own saddle and lead the small column out towards Rock Springs and Laramie's date with a hang rope.

9

Laramie felt uneasy. His chance of escape was near, but that opportunity, if taken, might also get him killed. It was not long into the afternoon and the mounted warriors who silently shadowed them had been there for the last two hours that he'd been aware of. They had stayed invisible for the most part, a flicker of movement further back in the forest which had caught his eye, the only thing that had given them away. He seemed to be the only one who knew they weren't alone.

The gunfighter couldn't understand how the Coltrains had not discovered that the Blackfeet were there. In country like this, acute awareness of your surroundings was essential for survival. Indians, wolves, mountain lions and grizzlies were prevalent throughout this region. Of all the things in the wilderness that could kill them, the Indians were their immediate threat.

Bo pricked his ears then tossed his head about. Even he knew they were there.

'Whoa boy,' Laramie soothed the big appaloosa. 'I know they're there.'

Shell Coltrain hipped in the saddle and snapped, 'What was that killer?'

'The horse said you stink and I agreed.'

'Laugh it up while you can Davis, we'll see who's laughing when you're on the gallows.'

'Knock it off back there,' Jeb Coltrain yelled over his shoulder.

The Sheriff rode in front of Laramie, along with Jim Clancy, and Shell Coltrain. Behind the gunfighter came the judge, Clay Adams and Orson Blake. They had taken a different path along the valley where the river bisected the mountains, instead of going back over the ridge and past Lonesome's spread.

The posse was about to go through the narrow pass and had just entered a stand of spruce when there was a soft hiss in the air. An arrow sliced its way through Jim Clancy's throat, the shaft still vibrating, its flint head erupted on the other side, and blood dripped from its sharp point. He opened his mouth to scream but emitted only a gargled sound, followed by a rush of deep crimson which ran down his chin.

Another arrow streaked out of the nearby trees and punched into his chest. This one ended his suffering and he fell from his horse to the ground with a thud.

'Indians!' shouted the judge. 'They've got Jim.'

Hot on the heels of the judge's cry, rifle fire opened up from behind them. Lead buzzed around the rider's heads like angry hornets. A cry behind Laramie told him that someone else was hit. He looked around and saw the young cow hand, Clay Adams slumped over his saddle horn.

The next one down was Orson Blake. His head appeared to explode as a heavy calibre bullet from an old Spencer carbine, hit him in the temple and blew out a fist sized hole as it exited. Blake toppled sideways from his horse.

Suddenly, ten Blackfoot warriors thundered out of the trees on horseback, the air filled with their blood curdling war cries.

Jeb Coltrain pulled his pistol and fired three shots at the oncoming horde, two went wild and the third pitched a brave from the back of his pony. Next to the Sheriff, Shell also loosed shots at the bare-chested horsemen.

The judge took one look at the charging Indians and spurred his mount hard and bolted past Laramie. Jeb Coltrain called out as his brother's horse narrowly missed his own, but the fleeing man didn't slow. He galloped hard along the trail, clods of damp earth flicked into the air by flying hooves as he went.

Clay Adams, though grievously wounded, found the strength to get his horse moving and followed the judge on his wild ride. He swayed in the saddle, both hands locked onto the pommel in a voice like grip.

'God, damn it!' cursed Jeb Coltrain and fired off another two shots. 'Let's go!'

Shell followed close behind as the sheriff hauled round on the reins and kicked his horse into a gallop.

It was now or never. Using pressure through his legs, Laramie sent a message to the Appaloosa who responded instantly. Bo veered off the trail and plunged into the forest. He galloped sure footed across the uneven ground, dodging around rocks and trees.

A low branch administered a stinging flick across Laramie's face and immediately raised an angry welt. The blow made his eyes water and he tried to blink the tears away. War cries from his pursuers became louder as they closed the gap.

Laramie cast a glance back over his shoulder and saw three Blackfeet, with painted faces, as they tried hard to ride him down. He gave Bo a small kick and the Appaloosa found more speed as he broke out into a small, half acre clearing, the other side of which was a fifty-foot-high sheer rock wall.

'Ahh hell,' Laramie cursed aloud.

His choices were either left, or right? A quick glance in both directions made him none the wiser.

Bo had covered the ground quickly and the rock wall loomed large and grey in front of them. Left, or Right?

Damn it, Laramie choose! He chose left and knew immediately that it was a mistake.

An Indian, riding what was known as a Buffalo Horse, cannoned into Bo, and caused the big horse to go down and spill Laramie from the saddle. Unharmed, Bo was quick to regain his feet and waited for the gunfighter to climb back aboard.

A little shaken, Laramie struggled to his feet only to crash back to the ground with a Blackfoot warrior on top of him.

Air rushed from his lungs when he fell and he gasped for breath as the Indian's weight lay heavy on his chest.

Laramie fought hard against the semi naked man, the smell of bear grease filled his nostrils. They rolled about, two gladiators in a fight to the death. The life and death struggle finished when Laramie felt something sharp prick the skin of his neck and he froze. The Indian had a razor-sharp knife to his throat.

The gunfighter lay there and looked up into the black, hate filled eyes of the warrior. Both men breathed heavily from their exertions.

'If you try to fight, I will kill you,' the Blackfoot hissed.

* * *

'God, damn it Jeb, you let the murdering son of a bitch get away!' Judge Zebulon Coltrain raged at his brother.

'In case you didn't notice brother,'

the Sheriff snarled back, 'I was kinda busy!'

The remnants of the posse had run for five miles after they'd lost the war party before a halt was called. Jim Clancy and Orson Blake had been lost in the bloody exchange. Clay Adams still clung to his saddle, the lower half of his body covered in blood. Shell Coltrain had a shallow graze from a bullet on his upper arm and the Sheriff's horse sported a laceration across its rump.

The judge, however, was unharmed and full of anger at the loss of his son's killer. 'You should have made sure that he was with you. He was your responsibility, you're the law.'

The judge paused before he continued his tirade, his voice ratcheted up a notch. 'And now we have to go back there and get him, all because you could not do your job!'

'How would you know what I was or wasn't doin', Judge. You was so busy runnin' like a damned rabbit, I'm surprised we caught up to you.'

'My horse bolted when the shooting started,' the judge spluttered in his defence. 'It took me all my time to get it stopped.'

Shell interrupted them. 'We need to get Clay to a doc. He's hurt real bad.'

'The hell we do!' the judge said with finality. 'He can come with us or he can stay here, but we don't leave these mountains without Jeremiah's murderer.'

Jeb Coltrain climbed off his horse and walked over to Clay Adams. 'How are you doin' Clay?'

Clay lifted his head and the Sheriff could easily see that the young cowboy was in a bad way. His face was pale and sweat soaked. Pain filled his eyes. 'I hurt bad Sheriff. My insides are on fire.'

Jeb lifted his hand and peeled back the blood-soaked flap of Clay's jacket. The bullet had gone in just above his buckle. He shook his head. 'It's not good Clay but don't worry, we'll get you to a doctor.'

'Damn you, we don't have time!' the judge snarled.

Before anyone could stop him, Judge Zebulon Coltrain drew his Webley revolver and shot Clay Adams twice in the chest. 'There, he's been tended to. Now come on, let's ride.'

The posse was down to three.

* * *

It was late in the day and the sun sat just above the jagged peaks of the snow-capped mountains when the Blackfeet arrived back at Black Elk's camp. They had tied Laramie behind a horse and forced him to walk all the way. Bo was led behind by another warrior who had learned the hard way that the big Appaloosa didn't take kindly to strangers.

The camp was on the bank of a wide creek, with crystal clear water that flowed swiftly over a rocky bottom of rounded stones. There were somewhere near forty tepees scattered around the site and the small community turned out to watch as Laramie was paraded through it.

The tepees were constructed with a four-main pole frame work, with another dozen or more laid against these to complete the skeleton of the structure. All were lashed firmly into place before the hides were stretched over it and affixed.

They stopped outside a large tepee located near the centre of the encampment. A tall warrior stepped through the open flap and stared with contempt at the white prisoner. His skin was a deep bronze colour and his muscles rippled when he moved. His long, black hair was held off his face by a decorated headband and he wore deerskin leggings and a loin cloth. A necklace adorned with bear claws were testament to his bravery.

The Blackfoot brave who'd brought Laramie into camp spoke to this new warrior in a low voice. Laramie could not hear what was said but could guess that he was the subject of the conversation.

The Indian turned his attention back

to Laramie and asked in heavily accented English, 'Why are you in our land white man?'

'Your land? The last I heard the Blackfoot tribe were people of the plains.'

'It is not by choice we are here,' the Indian stated.

'Then it seems we have something in common.'

The warrior's dark eyes glittered. 'You have nothing in common with Black Elk or my people.'

Laramie shrugged. 'More than you think.'

Black Elk remained silent.

Laramie knew that he would only get one chance to be able to convince Black Elk that Laramie alive was better than him dead.

'I know that you seek the men who killed your brother and his woman.'

'How do you know this?' Black Elk hissed.

'Because I am after the same men,' Laramie explained.

Black Elk motioned the brave forward who'd brought the gunfighter into camp. The two conversed for a moment before the Blackfoot chief addressed Laramie.

'You were with the men who wore the shiny badges. The ones who killed my warriors at the place where the wagons change horses.'

'Did he also tell you that my hands were tied?' Laramie asked.

Black Elk nodded. 'Why?'

'I killed a man. He was no good and wanted to steal my horse.'

'If what you say is true, why should I believe you?' the chief asked sceptically.

'The men you seek killed my friend, the old man who lived alone in the valley of the *Ksisk-staki*, the beaver.'

Black Elk nodded to a couple of his braves and they turned and ran off.

'You speak our language,' observed the Blackfoot chief.

Laramie nodded. 'I picked up a little in my travels.'

'Tell me more about these men you

speak of and then I will decide what to do with you.'

Laramie noticed that Black Elk's hostility had waned some but the suspicion was still present. At least he was still alive, which was the main thing.

'They are led by a man called Blackie Harbin. He is a wanted killer by the white man's law. There is a young one with him called Benny, he's mean even though he's a kid. Two others ride with him, a man called Cato and a Crow, he's called Lone Wolf. The others are dead.'

'Do you know where they have gone?' Black Elk asked expectantly.

Laramie nodded. 'I think so.'

'Then you will tell me now,' the chief snapped.

The gunfighter shook his head. 'No, but I will take you.'

Black Elk was annoyed with his answer and it showed. He stepped forward swiftly and took out a wickedly sharp knife from the sheath at his narrow waist. He placed the knife at Laramie's throat.

'You will tell me white man or you will be made speak, the choice is yours.'

Laramie pushed it just a little further. 'After I tell you, I go with you.'

'Why, because he killed your friend?'

'There is another reason,' the gun-fighter confessed.

'What is it?' asked the chief as he withdrew the knife.

'There is a woman with the gang,' Laramie told Black Elk. 'She was on the stage the gang stopped. I took her away from them but now they have her back. The last thing I told her was that I was goin' to come get her.'

He waited for the Indian to digest the information he'd been given.

Black Elk nodded. 'Tell me where.'

10

The Coltrains made camp that evening deep amongst a stand of firs, well off the trail so the flickering, orange flames of the small fire would not be visible.

Earlier, they had returned to the scene of the Blackfoot ambush and found nothing other than their dead comrades. They had discussed a burial but Jeb had refused. If the Blackfeet returned, he didn't want them to find freshly turned earth. There was no sign of Laramie and they'd spent a few cautious hours trying to pick up his trail, without success. With darkness upon them now, they did the only thing left to do and made camp for the night.

'What are we goin' to do now Uncle Jeb?' asked Shell Coltrain, who tossed a small stick onto the fire.

The Sheriff shrugged his shoulders. 'Don't rightly know Shell. Davis could be anywhere in these mountains by now.'

'We keep looking,' asserted the judge. 'Come sun up tomorrow, we search for him until he is found.'

'Sure Zeb, why not?' the Sheriff agreed sarcastically. 'We'll just keep traipsin' all over these mountains, just the three of us, with all them Indians tryin' to lift our hair, especially when we know just where to find him don't we?'

'What about the girl?' Shell interrupted.

'What about her?' questioned his uncle.

'Do you think he would go after her?'

'It's possible I guess,' the sheriff conceded. 'But she's gone off with Harbin and God alone knows where that is.'

'I know,' said Shell confidently. 'I overheard them talkin' and they've a hideout over by Eagle falls.'

'Do you think you can find it?' asked his father.

Shell looked at the judge and saw the renewed hope in his face. 'Sure, at least I think I can.'

The judge looked across the fire at his brother. 'How far is it to Eagle falls?'

'A day and a bit in this country,' Jeb Coltrain confirmed.

'Have you been there before?'

'Yeah, but it's the first I've heard about some sort of hideout bein' over that way though.'

'It's there I tell you,' Shell insisted. 'I heard 'em talkin''

'Alright then,' said the sheriff. 'We'll do that.'

★ ★ ★

The outlaws sat about an old, scarred wooden table, piled with the stolen money from the stage.

'What are we goin' to do with the girl, Blackie?' Cato asked warily.

'I don't know, let me think about it for a day or so,' the outlaw leader

154

answered as he counted out the cash.

'Do you think she's worth anythin'?' asked Benny.

Harbin shrugged. 'Maybe, we can try I guess, but I want you boys to leave her alone for the time being.'

'Hell Blackie, can't we just have a little fun?' begged Benny.

'I said no. If any of you touch her,' Harbin paused and stared unflinchingly at Benny. 'I'll damn well shoot you.'

Sally was in the only other room that the roughhewn log cabin possessed and had heard everything that the outlaws said. In a way she was relieved, for the moment. She wasn't sure what would happen after that. What would the outlaws do to her?

They had arrived at the cabin late in the afternoon, just before dark and she'd been locked away in the room ever since. It was small, dark and smelt like a skunk had died in it, but if it was where Blackie Harbin slept, she could understand why it had that peculiar odour.

Sally tried not to think of the bad things that could happen to her. She wanted to stay positive and focus on the one chance she knew she had. That one hope that had been taken away to be hanged for killing a man. The more Sally thought about her predicament, the more she thought she had no hope at all.

Raucous laughter from the next room brought Sally back to the present. She looked at the door, old, gap ridden and grey with age. More laughter, this time much louder.

'I'll come after you,' Laramie's words echoed in her head.

Hopefully, he would come soon.

★   ★   ★

The following afternoon, Black Elk and Laramie sat on their horses, hidden from sight in a dense thicket of Spruce.

'Do you see the tall tree?' asked the Indian Chief as he pointed to a Cedar next to a large rock monolith.

Laramie nodded. 'I see it.'

'Young Deer told me that an entrance lies beyond the rock beside it. There were many tracks going in and out. It seems you tell the truth.'

A flood of relief washed over Laramie at the news. 'What do you want to do now?'

'We will wait for dark and then go into the canyon,' said Black Elk.

'And then what?'

'Then we wait.'

Two hours after the sun went down, Laramie, Black Elk and ten other warriors entered the box canyon. Laramie was apprehensive about the outcome, once the Indians attacked the cabin. He tried to get Black Elk to allow him to try to get Sally out before the attack but he would not hear of it.

'She will have to take her chances,' the Indian said coldly. 'But if she dies, it will not be by the hand of one of my warriors.'

Laramie made up his mind that once the battle started, he would somehow get Sally to safety.

'I want a gun,' Laramie insisted.

Black Elk stared at the gunfighter in silence.

'I aim to get the woman when the battle starts, and to do that I need a gun,' Laramie explained.

'What about the man you have come to kill?'

'For me, the woman comes first.'

Black Elk nodded and signalled to a brave. 'Take Coyote Man's rifle.'

The Indian gave Laramie his old Henry. It had seen better days, and the stock was pitted and scratched, but it was clean so he guessed it wouldn't blow up in his face when he fired it. He emptied the magazine and found that it was fully loaded. Then he thumbed the bullets back in and worked the lever to put one back in the breech.

The soon to be attackers surrounded the run-down cabin. Horses were in a makeshift corral but the Indian braves were so skilled in what they did, not one stirred or nickered in alarm. Once in position, a chorus of night bird calls drifted through the canyon on the light mountain breeze.

'My warriors are ready,' Black Elk confirmed.

Now they had to wait.

* * *

'I need to go outside,' said Sally.

Blackie Harbin raised his eyebrows in genuine surprise. 'What, again?'

'Yes, again.'

'Girl, you just don't stop do you,' Harbin grouched. 'Damn it to hell. Cato take her out.'

'Aww, why me Blackie?' Cato complained.

'Because it's your turn, now take her out damn it,' Harbin ordered. 'And keep an eye on her. These trips outside is becoming too frequent.'

Cato rose from where he sat with the others as they played poker to pass the time. It was probably a good thing that he was forced to take a break because he was on a hot losing streak and his pile of money had dwindled fast. If the queen high hand he now had was any indication, it wasn't going to get any better.

The outlaw opened the door and stepped aside to allow Sally to pass. Once through, Sally went around the side of the cabin and out back where there was a small patch of brush she could use for privacy. The cold made her shiver.

'Hurry it up,' Cato urged. 'I got a game to get back to.'

Sally ignored him.

'Did you hear me?'

Sally rolled her eyes at the outlaw's impatience. 'I hear you.'

Cato mumbled something under his breath that she couldn't make out.

With her business finished, Sally was about to step from behind the bush when a feint whisper behind her drew her attention, then a muscular arm snaked out of the darkness and a hand fastened over her mouth.

Her scream was immediately stifled as another arm wrapped around her body. A strong smell permeated her nostrils as she struggled against the vice like grip.

A heavily accented voice sounded close to her ear. 'Don't fight, I help.'

It took a moment for Sally to realise what the speaker had said, and she struggled against the unbreakable grip a little longer.

The voice spoke again, 'Don't fight, I help.'

Sally stilled herself and the voice said, 'Come with me.'

★　★　★

'Are you finished yet or what?' Cato asked, his impatience evident.

There was no reply from the other side of the bush.

'Ma'am, are you finished?' This time his voice held a different tone. That of concern. Not for the woman, but for himself.

An internal conflict started to rage

inside of Cato. 'Ma'am, I asked if you were finished?'

No answer or movement. Cato couldn't wait any longer, he had to know. His pulse quickened and a bead of sweat formed on his brow. Cato stepped around the brush.

And found nothing. Sally was gone. Harbin was going to kill him for letting her get away. His gaze raked the enshrouding darkness in the hope that she would appear. Just walk out into the light and make it all better. Then he wouldn't have to tell Blackie.

'She's gone,' Cato said, his head hung low like a school boy about to be scolded by the teacher.

'She's what?' Blackie Harbin exploded.

'I'm sorry Blackie, she's gone,' Cato explained sheepishly. 'One minute she was there and then the next she was gone.'

'God, damn it!' Harbin cursed, as his face turned crimson. 'One simple job. Take her outside and keep an eye on her. How hard can it be?'

'But I was watching' her.'

'Yeah, sure,' came Harbin's sarcastic reply. 'That's why you're in here and she's out there. Sometimes I wonder whether any of you men have a damn brain between you.'

Cato made for the door.

'Where are you goin'? Harbin asked.

'Out to look for her,' said Cato.

Blackie shook his head. 'No, stay here. Lone Wolf you go.'

The Crow disappeared out the door.

'You better hope he finds her,' Harbin warned. 'For your sake.'

A cold chill ran down Cato's spine.

★ ★ ★

'Laramie, you're here,' Sally's voice was a mixture of relief and happiness as she threw her arms around him.

'Did you ever doubt that I would come?' he said, embarrassed and tried to extricate himself from her embrace.

She let him go, aware of his unease. 'I'm not sure what I expected.'

'Are all of the bad men still there?' Black Elk asked as he abruptly interrupted the reunion.

Sally looked at the big Blackfoot chief and then back to Laramie. 'It's okay, if it wasn't for Black Elk, you would still be with Harbin.'

'Yes,' Sally confirmed.

'Would it be possible to get her out of here before the fighting starts?' Laramie asked hopefully.

Black Elk thought for a moment and then nodded. 'I will have Leaning Bear take her back to our camp. My woman will look after her.'

'I don't want to go,' Sally protested.

'You'll be safer there, they will take care of you.' Laramie reassured her. 'After we are done here, I'll come and get you and take you to your father.'

'I'm not sure . . . '

'Just do it,' he said more forcefully. 'I need to do this for Lonesome.'

'Okay,' she agreed reluctantly and turned to leave.

A short time later Sally was gone

with her Blackfoot escort.

Laramie turned to Black Elk, 'If anythin' happens to me can you . . . '

'Yes,' the Chief said deadpan. 'I will make her my second wife.'

'What?'

'White man humour,' Black Elk explained. 'She will be returned to her people.'

* * *

'Well, where is she?' Blackie Harbin asked Lone Wolf.

'I don't know.'

'Damn it Cato, I told you to keep an eye on her,' Harbin's temper rose and his hand drifted toward one of his pearl handled gun-butts.

'Wait,' said Lone Wolf. 'Before you decide you want to shoot someone, you need to know we are surrounded by Blackfeet.'

Cato turned pale. 'Aww hell, we're dead.'

Harbin remained quiet, a hundred

things flicked through his mind.

Benny on the other hand, smiled. He checked the loads in his new Remingtons and said almost gleefully, 'Let's kill us some Indians.'

Blackie's eyes darted across to Benny. 'Hold on kid, don't be in such a rush to die.'

'Who's goin' to die?' he said cockily. 'I sure as hell ain't, I got too much livin' to do. Besides, I ain't famous yet.'

Blackie looked hard at Lone Wolf. 'Are you sure we're totally surrounded?'

The Crow nodded.

'Are the horses still there?' Blackie asked hopefully.

'Yes.'

'What are we goin' to do?' asked an ashen faced Cato.

'Well the way I figure it,' said Harbin confidently, 'is they have the girl. And they'll be expectin' us to come out lookin' for her.'

'Yeah, but we ain't goin' to do that right?' Cato asked hesitantly.

'That's exactly what we're goin to

do,' the boss outlaw confirmed. 'It wouldn't look right if we didn't.'

'They'll kill us if we go out there. Pick us off one by one,' Lone wolf stated the obvious.

Harbin ignored the comment and continued, 'We'll get into the corral and take the horses on outta here. Don't worry about saddlin' 'em, just jump on 'em and light out. They won't be expectin' it and in all the confusion we'll be able to get away.'

Not one person in the room believed what was said. Not even Harbin himself.

★   ★   ★

Laramie and Black Elk watched as the outlaws came out of the cabin. They divided into pairs then split up. One pair walked towards the corral while the others circled around to the back of the cabin.

'They look for the woman,' Black Elk observed.

167

Laramie wasn't so sure. One of the outlaws in the first group acted kind of nervous. He glanced around as though he expected something to happen. And then a false bird call tipped the situation over the edge.

The outlaw drew his gun and fired off into the darkness.

'They know we're here!' yelled Laramie. 'They're going for the horses.'

A chorus of cries broke out in the darkness, followed by more gunfire. Laramie and Black Elk moved forward from the trees but hurried gunshots flew over their heads and made them take cover.

'They're firing wild,' the gunfighter called to the Indian.

There was a disturbance in the corral as the outlaws climbed upon the backs of their horses. More gunfire sounded and a Blackfoot warrior cried out in pain. There was yelling from the corral and the horses surged forward and busted through the lodge pole rails.

Two men rode the gauntlet of fire

laid down by the Blackfeet. Laramie raised the Henry rifle and fired. The shot missed so he levered and fired again. This time the lead rider threw up his arms and toppled from his saddle. He tried to rise, but from the darkness two warriors emerged and one lunged at the fallen man with a knife.

The second rider almost made it but his horse stumbled and went down. It had clipped a fallen log which caused it to land awkwardly and it snapped its right foreleg. The night was pierced with the animal's high pitched squeal of pain. Its rider lunged to his feet and started to fire wildly into the dark until the hammer of his gun clicked onto an empty chamber.

There was an audible thunk beside Laramie, and Black Elk emitted a low grunt and crumpled to the ground. The gunfighter checked the Indian who gasped, 'Get them, don't let them escape.'

Meanwhile the outlaw tried hurriedly to reload his gun, but to no avail. An arrow streaked from the darkness and pierced his chest. It was followed by two more and silently, the man dropped his gun and slowly sank to the earth.

That left two more, thought Laramie, but where were they?

* * *

When the shooting started, Blackie Harbin and Benny were behind the old cabin and were no longer sure whether to head back inside or toward the corral.

'God, damn it,' cursed Harbin. 'That's torn it.'

Benny ducked low, ready to run for the horses.

Harbin stopped him as he blocked the way with his arm. 'Wait.'

Out of the darkness loomed a Blackfoot brave who carried a bow. Harbin raised his gun and shot the approaching man twice. The Indian dropped to the ground without a sound as another came at the pair. This one was armed with a rifle which he fired at them. Benny and Harbin both fired at the warrior and he was flung backwards by the heavy impact of the bullets. He went down and never moved.

'Follow me kid,' Blackie urged as he pointed in the direction the Indians had come from, 'We're goin' this way.'

'What about the horses?'

'We'd never make it,' Harbin declared. 'Now come on.'

'But Blackie,' Benny protested, 'we can't get out that way.'

'I know, but we can get in behind the Blackfeet and maybe slip out. Now come on while they are still busy with the other two.'

So, the two outlaws slipped into the night and left their comrades to die.

★ ★ ★

The sun poked its head over the mountains and its rays caressed the land like warm fingers. Laramie looked down at the bodies of Cato and Lone

Wolf. Once the Blackfeet had finished with them, they were a grizzly sight.

'What about the other two?' Black Elk asked Laramie with gritted teeth as another wave of pain swept over him. The stray bullet had taken him low in his chest. How it had not hit anything vital was beyond Laramie, but there was no way that he could ride a horse, so was being transported back to his village on a travois.

'They got away, but will not get far. They have no horses so will be easy to find.'

'You must find them,' the Chief hissed. 'Find them and bring them back to me, alive if possible.'

'And what if I can't bring them in alive?'

'Then dead will do, but I want to see the bodies of the men who killed my brother.'

Laramie watched as the Blackfeet disappeared with their Chief, the travois cut furrows in the earth as it was dragged along behind Black Elk's Palomino.

The gunfighter walked across to Bo and the big Appaloosa nuzzled his shoulder. 'We got us some killers to track down boy, are you ready to go.'

Bo tossed his head about and snorted.

'Yeah, I thought so, come on then.'

Laramie adjusted the unfamiliar weight of Cato's holstered gun before he climbed up into the saddle and rode out after Blackie Harbin and the killer kid, Benny.

11

Two hours after Laramie and the Blackfeet had left the hideout, the Coltrains arrived. Cato and Lone Wolf had been left in the open and the birds and other wildlife had started to strip meat from the bodies.

The judge took one look and placed a white handkerchief over his mouth to stop the rise of bile. Shell on the other hand, took one look at the mauled bodies, and lost his breakfast.

'Jesus Shell,' cursed the Sheriff, 'if you're goin' to do that, take it somewhere else.'

Jeb Coltrain dismounted and looked around. He stooped and picked up an arrow that stuck out of the soft ground. 'Looks like the Blackfeet got here before us.'

He snapped the arrow in two and cast it aside. The Sheriff looked around some more and took in the macabre landscape, but knew it was a waste of time.

'What now?' asked Shell Coltrain.

'We keep damn well looking,' snapped the judge.

'Hold on there Zeb, just think on it a minute,' the Sheriff cautioned his brother. 'Like I told you last time, we can traipse around these mountains for days and find nothin' and now, with the Indians on the war path, we'd probably end up with our scalps hangin' in some brave's tepee. Otherwise, we can head for the place where Davis is goin' to end up anyway, if he's still alive.'

'What do you mean, Jeb?' asked the judge, seemingly ready to listen to reason.

'We know Davis is after the woman,' Jeb continued to explain. 'Now if he gets her back, he's goin' to end up in Mountain Pass, and if he does, we'll be there waitin' for him.'

He waited while his brother digested the information. 'That's all well and good but what if he doesn't turn up in

Mountain Pass.'

'Then he'll be dead,' the Sheriff said matter of factly. 'It's that simple.'

'Alright we'll do it your way,' the judge conceded.

The three remaining posse men rode out and left the carrion eaters to their feast.

★   ★   ★

Laramie caught up with the outlaws shortly after noon. He'd been on the killer's trail for half a day but they hadn't made it easy. The men had stuck to rough terrain which made it difficult for horses to traverse and anyone to track them. Many times, Laramie had to dismount and look for sign in amongst the rocky landscape.

The trail lead him past a place he knew as White Falls, then up over a ridge line and along an escarpment before it dropped down to an expanse of water known as Miller's Pond.

It was here that Laramie found

Benny, as he sat on the pond's rocky shoreline, waiting. Laramie halted Bo ten yards from him. The gunfighter was instantly wary and cocked the hammer of the Henry he had laid across his lap.

He climbed down and moved away from the big Appaloosa to keep him out of harm's way.

'Howdy kid,' Laramie greeted, 'didn't expect to find you here alone.'

Benny looked at Laramie, impressed to see the gunfighter. 'Blackie said it was you. He saw you comin' down off the escarpment.'

Laramie looked around, concerned about what Benny had told him. 'Where is Harbin, kid?'

He waved a hand in the air. 'He's around here somewhere. He promised me I could have first crack at you.'

'What happens after you go down kid?' the gunfighter asked, his face expressionless. 'Is he waitin' to bush-whack me?'

The kid's eyes darted left to a thick grove of Aspen. It was just a flicker, but was enough to tell Laramie that that was where Harbin was hidden and waiting for the right time to pull the trigger.

'What makes you think I will be the one to go down? You're mighty confident of yourself.'

Laramie watched silently as the kid climbed to his feet and stood in front of him with his feet spread shoulder width apart.

'Are you ready to die old man?'

'You talk too much kid,' said Laramie flatly.

Benny ignored the remark and continued to talk. 'You know the funny thing about this? It's the fact that when I kill you, it'll be your guns that do it. It'll be your guns that finally bring about your demise. Now isn't that ironic?'

Laramie knew he faced a stacked deck. The two outlaws held the advantage, so it was time to show some initiative and take it back.

'Like I said kid, you talk too much.'

Without warning, Laramie swung the Henry up and levelled it at Benny's middle. The whiplash of the shot echoed through the air that surrounded Miller's Pond. Benny's mouth opened in shock as the .44 calibre slug tore into his gut. Laramie knew instantly that the kid was out of the fight and moved swiftly to find cover.

The sound of another shot rang across the pond and a bullet burned through the air close to Laramie's head. He tried desperately to make himself as hard a target as possible then ran as fast as he could.

Harbin fired again and the slug sent up a small geyser of dirt at Laramie's feet. He darted to the left, and dived behind a dead fall tree, large enough to conceal his bulk.

He lay there for a moment and gulped down large breaths of air. Harbin fired again and splinters flew from the tree. The gunfighter eased up, just high enough to peek to see if he could locate Blackie Harbin's position.

The outlaw fired again and more splinters flew. The gunfighter ducked back down. 'I got you now.'

Blackie Harbin was back in amongst the Aspen, beside a stump of a fallen tree he used as cover. He was crouched down on one knee, armed only with his pearl handled Colts. Laramie appeared up over the dead fall and worked the Henry furiously. He fired and levered until the Henry was empty, then he leapt over his cover and ran for the trees.

The hail storm of lead caused Harbin to throw himself down on the damp earth as an evasive tactic. Angry cracks sounded above his head as the bullets passed close.

'Damn, son of a bitch,' he cursed loudly.

After the flurry of shots had stopped, Harbin rose and brushed furiously at the hair that hung in his face. He spat little bits of grass from his mouth that had been forced in by the sudden dive to earth in his attempt to avoid death.

He caught sight of Laramie who ran towards the tree line. He raised his Colt and fired twice, both bullets missed, although one tore a hole in the gun-fighter's jacket. Harbin took aim again but this time the hammer fell on an expended chamber.

'Damn it,' the outlaw cursed again and brought up his other Colt, but was too late. Laramie had found the safety of the trees.

Once inside the Aspen, Laramie dived to the ground among the tall grass that grew there and drew the six-gun he'd taken from Cato's corpse. Laramie double checked the loads just to make sure they were all fine, then stealthily moved to circle Blackie Harbin's position until he could get a bead on him.

'I'm not surprised you're here Laramie. I just knew that posse wouldn't stop you,' Harbin called out. 'I saw it in your eyes just before we rode out with the girl.'

Laramie ceased movement to listen as Harbin continued, 'I don't have the girl, by the way. I think the Indians have her, so good luck gettin' her back from them.'

'I'm here after you Blackie, the girl's fine. You don't have to worry about her, just me,' Laramie informed the outlaw.

The penny dropped. 'You were there at the cabin? Were you there with them red devils?'

'I was there. How do you think they found you?' the gunfighter informed him. 'Slate told me about the hideout. That's how I knew where you'd gone.'

'You sold us out to damned Indians, you son of a bitch! What white man does that?' asked Harbin in a snarled voice.

'I don't know Blackie, but tell me, what kind of man rides around rapin' and killin' women?' Laramie countered.

'She was a damned redskin. She don't count.'

The gunfighter shook his head in disbelief. 'She was a woman, and it don't matter what colour her skin was.'

'So, what now?' Harbin inquired.

'You plan on tryin' to kill me over an Indian woman?'

'Nope, the Indians want you for that. Me, I want you for killin' my friend.'

'You mean that double crossin' son of a bitch, Slate?' Harbin asked surprised.

'Nope, the old mountain man you shot at the cabin,' the gunfighter answered.

'Oh hell, him?' the outlaw said non-plussed. 'He was about dead anyway. I did him a favour by shootin' him. 'I'll give him one thing though, he was one tough rooster.'

The conversation died off for a moment before Harbin came to a decision. 'Hey Laramie?'

'Yeah, what?'

'I'm comin' out,' the outlaw informed him.

Laramie watched from his hiding position as Harbin stood and walked out into the open, hands raised at shoulder height. He noticed too, that Harbin had left his Peacemakers in their holsters. Laramie came erect and holstered the Colt. Both men watched each other warily as they emerged from the Aspen and crunched across the gravel at the pond's shore.

'Do you think right here is good enough Mister Legend?' Harbin asked as he stopped and went into a gunfighter's stance.

Laramie was emotionless. 'Sure, why not. Guess it don't matter much where you die.'

Blackie Harbin gave Laramie a wry smile. 'Guess it don't.'

Hands blurred as they dove for guns. Harbin's Peacemaker came out and roared a hair's breadth before Laramie's. Two gunshots blended as one. Harbin's bullet gouged a red furrow on the outside of the gunfighter's left shoulder and caused a small spray of blood to erupt from the shallow wound.

In the fraction of time that it took for this to happen, the bullet from Laramie's Colt hammered into the outlaw's chest and exploded out his back.

Harbin smiled at his killer. 'I beat you, you son . . . of a bitch. I damn well beat you. I told you I was . . . faster.'

Laramie watched as Blackie Harbin tried to say something more, but a flood of red welled up and spilled down his chin, his words a wet, gargled sound.

The gunfighter watched as Harbin took two steps and fell forward, dead.

Laramie stared at the prone figure of the outlaw for a time before the pain of his wound registered. He examined it and decided he would fix it up later. He walked over to where Benny lay in the gravel, dying. The shot had hit him six inches above his buckle and caused a wound from which he would not recover.

'I guess you're as good as what they say,' his voice wasn't much above a pain filled whisper.

Laramie shook his head. 'Just more careful kid.'

'I'm dyin' ain't I.' It was more a statement than a question.

'Yeah, kid, you're dyin',' Laramie confirmed what Benny already knew.

He coughed and asked Laramie for a favour.

Laramie didn't exactly know why he agreed to it, but he sat with Benny until death came. Even though the kid was a cold-blooded killer, dying alone was the one thing the gunfighter feared. For that reason, only, he waited patiently for him to pass.

When it was over, Laramie did something else he didn't really understand, and buried them. Blackie Harbin was interred with his twin Peacemakers, the killer's weapons deserved to be with their owner. Benny got the Colt that Laramie had taken from Cato.

With the familiar weight of the twin Remingtons about his waist, he felt whole again.

Bo waited patiently for him and when he mounted the big Appaloosa, he patted his neck and said, 'Let's go get the girl and take her home.'

★　★　★

When Sally had arrived at Black Elk's village, she was sequestered away in a large tepee. Even though she was in the middle of an Indian encampment, she felt safe.

The flap of the tepee was swept aside and a young Blackfoot woman, clothed in a deer skin dress, entered with a bowl of food which consisted mainly of deer meat.

She had long, sleek black hair that fell halfway down her back. She was slim built and of average height. Her hair framed a pretty face with soft, dark eyes set just the right distance apart. She smiled warmly at Sally and when she did, revealed perfectly even teeth.

Sally smiled back when the woman gave her the bowl. 'Thank you, it smells lovely.'

'It is deer. Eat it, while it is hot,' the woman said in halting English.

Sally held a hand flat against her chest and said, 'My name is Sally.'

'My name is Little Fawn.'

Sally smiled and tried her food, it tasted quite good and she told Little Fawn so.

When Sally had finished her meal, the squaw left her to rest. After the previous day's chaos, she lay on the buffalo robes that were provided, and slept.

Sometime later, Sally was awoken by a loud noise from outside the tepee. The flap was swept aside suddenly and two Blackfoot warriors helped a third inside. Sally recognised him immediately as the Indian, Black Elk.

He was wounded and she scrambled aside as he was laid down on the buffalo robes Sally had slept on. Little Fawn followed them in with a look of concern deeply etched on her face.

The two warriors left and Little Fawn started to tend to Black Elk. Sally moved over to get a better look.

'Can I help?' she asked Little Fawn

'Yes,' said Little Fawn. 'Keep hand here.'

She took Sally by the hand and placed it firmly over the wound. Sally felt Black Elk flinch and he said something in his native tongue that only the Indian woman could understand.

Little Fawn looked at Sally. 'I'll be back soon.'

After she had left, Sally asked, 'What Happened? Where is Laramie?'

Black Elk related to her the news of the battle with the outlaws, how he became wounded and that two of the outlaws had escaped.

'What about Laramie?'

'Do not worry, your man will be fine. He has gone after the ones who escaped.'

'What? Oh no,' Sally was taken aback. 'He's not my man. He just happened to be the one to risk his life and try to save me from those outlaws.'

'He is a good man, very strong, brave. He would make you a fine husband,' Black Elk asserted.

Before Sally could respond, Little Fawn came back into the tepee with a bowl of something that looked like mud. She put it on both sides of Black Elk's wound and bandaged him up.

When she finished with the bandage, she spoke to Black Elk again in their language. He frowned and looked at Sally. 'The man, Laramie, his friend the old one?'

'Yes, Lonesome, the old mountain man that Blackie Harbin killed,' Sally said with a puzzled frown.

'My woman says he still alive. He here in village.'

A rush of emotion flowed through Sally when she registered what Black Elk had said, 'Where is he? I must see him. Is he alright?'

Black Elk tried to rise. He bit back a cry of pain as his wound protested violently at the movement. His wife put a hand on his muscular chest to stop him from going any further. She shook her head and the Indian chief lay back down.

'Little Fawn will take you to him,' he conceded.

Sally followed the lithe woman out of the large tepee to another, smaller one. The Indian woman lifted the hide flap aside and allowed Sally to enter first. She let her eyes adjust to the dim light and looked around. She saw him then, where he sat by a small fire in the centre of the tepee.

He looked up at her, his face looked drawn but he smiled and said, 'Hell girl, ain't you a sight for these old eyes.'

12

It had taken twenty years for Mountain Pass to become what it was now. A town that had started life as, what its name suggested, a mountain pass. That was until late one afternoon, in the middle of summer, a weary traveller named John Brooks, had made camp on the site.

He laid out his bed roll on a flat piece of ground and turned in. All night long, whenever he rolled over, a small bulge dug into his side. After a long sleepless night, come morning he'd had enough. He packed up the bed roll and for good measure decided to take out his exhausted frustration on the damn rock that had caused him to lose so much sleep.

Brooks was about to throw it into the forest when a tiny glint, made by the morning sunlight, flashed off the rock and caused him to explore the thing further. What he saw made him stay at the pass for a further two weeks.

Gold!

He explored the bottom of the deep scars in the foot of the pass itself and the silt that washed down from the foothills at the base of the peaks. When he was finished, Brooks had two thousand dollars' worth of gold, in his saddle bags.

That was the beginning of the Mountain Pass gold rush. First came the miners and within one year, claims had sprung up all over. As the traders slowly arrived, the town began to emerge.

In the beginning, it was a town made of canvas tents, followed later by more permanent wooden structures. False front stores and other shops were in abundance along the main street and at one point, while the mines were at their peak, there were no less than twelve saloons.

It was a lawless time. Claim jumpers

were rife and gold shipments were stolen on a regular basis. Men died frequently by gunshot, knife wound or sickness. It was just a regular boom town.

Then law came and the gold dropped off. Miners left and were replaced by ranchers who cleared some of the surrounding land to raise cattle. Of the few claims that remained in the hills, only a couple still paid.

It was into this now peaceful, law abiding town that the Coltrains rode. Their horses were played out and the men were tired and hungry. They rode along the dusty main street until they found the livery stable with its large, red painted doors.

They tied their horses to the hitch rail out the front and walked in through the main double doors where they were greeted by a grizzled looking hostler.

'What can I do for you gents?' asked the middle-aged man dressed in bib-front overalls.

'We want to put our horses up for a

few days,' said Jeb Coltrain. 'There's three of 'em. Give them some good feed and a rub down.'

The hostler smiled a toothless smile and said, 'Sure gents, no problems. I got plenty of room now.'

While Jeb was talking to the hostler, Shell walked up and down the aisle and looked into the stalls to see if he could see Laramie's horse. When he finished, Shell looked at his kin and shook his head.

The Sheriff fixed his gaze once more on the hostler and opened his jacket so his badge could be clearly seen. 'Have you seen a feller ride into town at all on a big, chocolate coloured, Appaloosa stud? He'd most likely have a woman with him.'

The hostler's eyes lingered on the badge for a moment before he answered, 'Nope Sheriff, can't say's I have. Ridin' an Appaloosa you said?'

The Sheriff nodded. 'that's right.'

The man thought some more. Then, 'Nope, no one come through here like that. I'd remember if he did. What this feller done any ways?'

'He murdered my . . . ' the judge started before the sheriff cut him off.

'He killed my deputy over in Rock Springs,' Jeb Coltrain finished.

The hostler made a silent oh with his mouth, thought about what was just said and then, 'Say are you Sheriff Coltrain from over that way?'

'I am.'

The man smiled nervously. 'Hell, I sure am glad it's not my trail you're on. What's this feller's name so's I know who to look out for?'

'Laramie Davis,' answered Jeb Coltrain.

The hostler swallowed hard. 'The gunfighter?'

The judge grew impatient with all the questions. 'Yes damn it, the gunfighter.'

'Maybe I should get your payment in advance,' he said thoughtfully. 'He's the type of feller you go up against and don't come away from in one piece.'

The Sheriff stepped forward and

grabbed the hostler by the front of his overalls. 'Listen to me Mister, and you listen good. If you see him ride into town, you come and let me know pronto. If I find out you didn't, I'm goin' to come back here and burn the place down with you in it. Do you understand me?'

A cold sweat broke out over the man's brow and fear filled his eyes. 'Sure . . . sure thing, Sheriff. I understand.'

Jeb Coltrain pushed him away. 'Good, now take care of our horses.'

As the hostler watched the three men leave, he was filled with an escalated sense of foreboding that the quiet town of Mountain Pass was about to explode into violence.

* * *

The Coltrain's next stop was the Mountain Pass Sheriff's office. It was a double storey construction with an office downstairs and the jail cells located on the second floor. It had large glass windows out front and big yellow letters painted at the base of the second storey that said, JAIL.

Once inside, the three Coltrains found a tall, slim, young man with light coloured hair who sat behind a large cedar desk. Startled by their entrance, the man scrambled to his feet.

'What can I do for you fellers?' he asked nervously.

'Are you the Sheriff of this burg?' Jeb Coltrain asked.

'No, sir. I'm Deputy Gunderson, Lyle Gunderson.'

'Where's the Sheriff?' asked Jeb.

'He's out of town at the moment,' the deputy explained. 'The stage is late and his daughter was on it, so he took a posse out after it and left me in charge.'

The Sheriff of Rock Springs opened his jacket once more to display his badge. He showed no outward sign of any kind to tell he knew what had happened to the stage. 'The name's Coltrain, I'm from Rock Springs, this is

198

my brother Zeb, he's the local judge and this is his son Shell, my deputy.'

If there was any indication that the deputy had heard of the Coltrains, he didn't show it. 'So, what brings you over to our neck of the woods? Anythin' I can help you with?'

'We're trackin' a killer,' Jeb elaborated. 'We lost him in the mountains, but we're reasonably sure he's headed here.'

Concern showed on Gunderson's face. 'Who is this killer you're in pursuit of?'

'Laramie Davis,' answered the judge. 'He damn well killed my boy and I mean to see him hang for it.'

'He's ridin' a big Appaloosa, have you seen one in town at all?' asked Jeb Coltrain.

Gunderson shook his head. 'Nope, but man have you guys got a bear by the tail. I saw him in action once and let me tell you somethin', that man is lightning fast with a gun.'

'He'll be in hell when we're finished

with him,' asserted the judge.

'I wish you fellers luck in your endeavours,' Deputy Gunderson said politely. 'I'll let the undertaker know to be expectin' you.'

Jeb Coltrain moved swiftly and back handed Gunderson across the face. The blow was solid enough to knock the deputy to the hardwood floor. 'Don't you sass me boy. Let's get one thing straight from the start, Davis is comin' here and we are stayin' in town until he shows up. So just stay the hell out of our way.'

The three Coltrains left the Sheriff's office and stood out in the middle of the dusty main street.

'Where to now, Uncle Jeb?' Shell asked as he looked around.

'That place across the street looks mighty good, how about it?'

Shell looked across the street and saw what Jeb was talking about. In bright red letters on a well-kept building was painted the name, 'The Royal Flush Saloon'.

'I'll be in that,' Shell said with a smile. 'I could use a drink.'

'What about you, Judge? Are you comin'?' Jeb asked.

The judge looked at his brother and nodded. Jeb could see the hurt and rage in Zebulon's eyes and wondered how much more his brother could take before he cracked completely. Up until now, it was just a few chinks in his armour, but Jeb figured it wouldn't take much more.

Behind them, Deputy Gunderson stared out the big window of the Sheriff's office. He used a kerchief to dab at a small trickle of blood that ran from the corner of his bruised mouth. While he did that, he watched them walk across to The Royal Flush. There's a storm comin', he thought to himself, and the town is goin' to be right in the centre of it.

*   *   *

When Laramie arrived at the Blackfoot village the next day, he was greeted by

Black Elk who was now, against his wife's wishes, up and about.

'I see you are still alive *Mingan*,' Black Elk observed calling Laramie the Blackfoot name for Gray Wolf. 'What of men you hunted? Are they in spirit land?' Laramie nodded. 'The only spirit land they are in chief, is one filled with plenty of fire.'

'Where are bodies?' Black Elk enquired as the gunfighter climbed down from his saddle.

'I buried 'em,' Laramie said truthfully. 'If you want to see 'em you'll find their graves at a place the white men call Miller's Pond.'

'I know of it,' said Black Elk.

Laramie looked around. 'Where is the girl?

'She is with . . . ' It was as far as Black Elk got before Sally burst through the crowd of onlookers.

'Laramie!' she cried ecstatically. She grabbed his arm to prevent the embarrassment of a hug. 'I'm so glad you're okay.'

'Have they been lookin' after you girl?'

Sally nodded. 'Yes, they are wonderful people. They treated me very well indeed.'

'I'm glad,' the gunfighter said relieved.

She tugged on his arm. 'Come with me, I have a surprise for you.'

Laramie frowned at her strange behaviour, but followed Sally anyway. She took him to the tepee where she had spent most of her time, and out front, wrapped in a buffalo robe was that damned old Ridge Runner himself, Lonesome Lane.

'About time you damn well showed up, instead of gallivantin' around the countryside like some damn psalm singer,' Lonesome grouched.

Laramie couldn't believe it. He rubbed his eyes and looked again. 'You're meant to be dead.'

'Hell son, have you ever known a tough old boss loper like me to go under without a fight,' he said with a wry smile. 'Besides, I'd probably be dead if one of Black Elk's braves hadn't come along.'

Laramie remembered back to when he was first brought into camp, that when he related his story to the Blackfoot chief, the lone Indian had disappeared.

'It's good to see you still breathin' old man.'

'Did you get them fellers you went after Laramie?' Lonesome asked. 'I'm guessin' you did or you would still be out there huntin' 'em.'

'Yeah, they're gone. Folks won't have to worry about Blackie Harbin anymore,' Laramie went on to unfold the story to Lonesome and Sally.

'Good, saved me a job,' Lonesome said.

Laramie's expression grew serious. 'When we leave here you're comin' with us. There should be a doctor in Mountain Pass to give you the once over.'

'I'll be fine right here,' the old mountain man insisted.

'No arguments, you're comin' and that's it,' the gunfighter asserted

'What about the Coltrains?' Sally asked. 'They're still out there somewhere.'

'I'll talk to your Pa when we get to Mountain Pass, he might be able to sort somethin' out,' Laramie said hopefully.

'After everything you've done, I certainly hope so,' Sally said.

'Yeah, me too,' but he sounded less convinced.

★　★　★

The next day, they left the Blackfoot camp. Laramie rode Bo, while Sally and Lonesome rode a couple of Indian ponies they had been given. Hidden under Laramie's shirt was a necklace that Black Elk had given him. It was the one made of bear claws that the chief had worn and was for bravery. The Blackfoot chief figured that Laramie was going to need it more than he would.

13

Shortly after the sun went down, a woman's screams rang out through the saloon and brought Jeb Coltrain instantly to his feet. They originated from one of the many rooms at the top of the stairs, with doors that opened out onto the landing. More blood curdling screams brought a hushed silence to the bar.

'Aww hell!' snapped Jeb.

'What's up?' Shell asked, confused.

'Come with me,' said the older Coltrain as he hurried to the stairs.

The saloon owner beat him there and was half way up when Jeb put his foot on the first step.

The Rock Springs Sheriff turned to his nephew. 'Don't let anyone else up the stairs.'

'Sure,' answered Shell and drew his gun and turned to face the oncoming crowd. He cocked his six-gun and said firmly, 'Hold it right there folks. Ain't nothin' to see. Just go on back to your drinkin' and cards.'

Men hesitated for a moment, but confrontation with a cocked Colt was enough to make the bravest think twice. They all turned away except for a short, blonde whore. Mary had dull blue eyes and a full figure, which was trussed up into a bright red dress.

'I'm goin' up there,' she said, jaw set rigid in defiance.

Shell shook his head. 'Nope, Uncle Jeb said nobody else goes up.'

The look on Mary's face became more determined. 'The hell with him, I said I'm goin' up and I am. If you want to stop me then go ahead and shoot me.'

She shouldered past Shell and began to climb the stairs.

Shell couldn't hide the respect on his face. That was certainly some woman.

When Jeb Coltrain stopped outside the door that the screams came from, the saloon owner exclaimed, 'He's killing her! Do something!'

From the other side of the door came the loud smack of hand on flesh. It was quickly followed by more screams that pleaded, 'Stop. Please, stop.'

Jeb Coltrain tried the door but it was locked. 'Do you have a key?'

'There is only the one per door,' the saloon owner shook his head and answered hurriedly.

The Rock Springs Sheriff lifted his foot and with a mighty kick, the timber frame splintered and the door flew wide. The judge stood there semi-naked with a clenched fist raised, about to strike another blow.

'Judge, stop!' he cried.

But the judge punched the naked whore again in her already battered face. There was a sickening crunch as her jaw broke. She fell to the floor and whacked her head on the night table beside the rumpled bed. Mercifully for her, she was knocked unconscious and the pain of the last blow never really registered.

'How did you like that bitch?' crowed the judge as he stood over her prostrate form. 'You shouldn't of sassed me girl. I don't take to it; do you hear me? Damn whore.'

He raised his foot to kick her but his brother grasped him around the neck and threw him down on the bed. 'That's enough, Judge — you'll kill her. We don't need this right now.'

Jeb held the judge down as he fought to rise. 'Get the hell off me Jeb, I'm going to teach that bitch some more manners.'

'You've taught her enough, Judge. If you go teachin' her any more, them folks downstairs will have you strung up quick smart.'

Zeb Coltrain stopped his struggle and his brother let him go. 'Put your clothes on and get the hell out of here.'

While his brother got dressed, Jeb crouched beside the young woman to check her. She was alive, but the judge had really worked her over. Apart from the broken jaw, she had a busted nose, her left eye was already swollen shut, blood came from her split scalp courtesy of the night stand and as he looked at the bruises on her torso, he guessed she had broken ribs as well.

He looked up at the saloon owner. 'You'd best get her a doctor.'

The man ran from the room and was replaced immediately by the whore from downstairs, 'Oh my God, what happened?'

She looked at the judge. 'What the hell did you do to her you son of a bitch?'

Once more the judge's anger rose to the surface and he lunged at Mary. 'By hell, don't you start sassing me too. I'll give you what I gave her.'

Jeb Coltrain realised his brother had finally passed his tipping point. He rose from beside the unconscious woman, grabbed his brother's jacket by the lapels, and with all his strength pushed him out the door.

Using the momentum that he had, he ignored the judge's cries for him to stop, and shoved him along the landing to the top of the stairs. Once there, he stopped and looked his brother in the eye. 'You get the hell down those stairs and get yourself a drink. Then you find a table out of the way and stay there until I get this sorted. Do you understand me?'

Zebulon Coltrain looked into his brother's eyes and knew there was no arguing with Jeb. He'd seen that look before, usually just before he shot someone. His shoulders slumped. 'Sure Jeb. Okay I'll do it.'

Jeb Coltrain watched as his brother shuffled down the steps. His gaze then fell on his nephew at the bottom. 'Keep a damn eye on him.'

The Rock Springs Sheriff returned to the room and found Mary with the other whore cradled in her arms.

She looked at him with hate in her eyes.

'Why?' she asked, tears glistened as they streamed down her cheeks. 'Why did he have to do this to Ellie. She was kind and gentle. She wouldn't hurt anyone.'

Jeb didn't have time to answer before the Mountain Pass doctor brushed past him and knelt beside both women.

Jeb heard him say softly, 'Dear Lord.'

The doctor looked at her for a few minutes and said, 'We must get her to my office so I can examine her properly.'

'I'll get you some help,' offered the saloon keeper.

Jeb followed the Saloon owner out, who then organised men to help the doctor. He found the table where his brother and nephew were seated and sat down.

'How's the whore?' the judge asked with genuine concern. 'Is she going to be alright?'

'It's a bit damned late to be worryin' about that now ain't it,' Jeb said caustically. 'What the hell were you thinkin'? We're not in Rock Springs now.'

'Yes, well it's done, now isn't it?' the

judge bit back at his brother's attack. 'I told you she shouldn't have sassed me.'

Jeb Coltrain remained silent as he watched Deputy Gunderson come into the saloon and walk steadily up the stairs, then watched as the still unconscious Ellie was carried down them and out of the saloon and off to the doctor's office.

A brief time later, Gunderson came back downstairs with the saloon owner.

'Whatever happens, Judge, just follow my lead,' the Rock Springs Sheriff said quietly.

The judge gave his brother a questioning look. 'What?'

Jeb watched as Deputy Gunderson hesitated at first, then weaved his way through the tables and town's people to get to where the Coltrains were seated.

'What can we do for you Deputy?' asked Jeb Coltrain.

'I've come for your brother,' Gunderson said uneasily. 'I know he's a judge and all, but he shouldn't of wailed the tar outta that whore like he did.'

'Do you reckon you'll get him out of here, Deputy?' Shell sneered.

'Let it go Shell,' Jeb cautioned. 'Your Pa done wrong and a spell in jail might do him some good.'

Zeb Coltrain's jaw dropped. 'What the hell Jeb?'

'Shut it Zebulon,' Jeb hissed. 'Now hand over the Webley.

The judge reached slowly into his jacket and pulled his pistol out with two fingers. He handed it over with little fuss.

'Thank you Mister Coltrain,' Gunderson said, as relief flooded his face. 'A little bit of professional courtesy goes a long way.'

'No problem, Deputy. Do you mind if I come along with you?' Jeb asked innocently.

'Well . . . ' Gunderson started.

'It's just to see he doesn't give you any more trouble,' Jeb explained.

The deputy still wasn't sure. He had images in his head of the events that had occurred in the jail when the

Coltrains first arrived.

The owner of The Royal Flush could see the deputy's apprehension and stepped forward. 'I'll come with you Lyle.'

The anxiety left Gunderson with those simple words. 'Thanks Bob.'

Jeb Coltrain cursed quietly under his breath.

Gunderson drew his pistol from its holster and pointed it at his prisoner. 'If you'll step this way, Judge.'

'Before you go Deputy,' said Jeb Coltrain.

'What is it Mister Coltrain?'

'Zeb, how much money you got?'

The judge pulled out a wad of cash from his inside pocket and gave it to his brother.

'One more thing Gunderson, do you have a local judge or circuit?'

'Local, why?' Gunderson asked.

'Just curious,' Jeb answered.

'Are you comin' or not?' the deputy asked.

'Nope,' said the Rock Springs sheriff.

'I changed my mind.'

Gunderson shrugged his shoulders and took Zeb Coltrain off to jail.

'What are you up to?' Shell asked his Uncle. 'We can't just let them lock Pa up.'

'We're not, I'm goin' to see the local judge.'

* * *

'I don't understand your honour, you want me to let him out?' Gunderson was confused.

'That's what I said Lyle. Let the good judge out.'

'But he beat Ellie half to death,' Gunderson protested.

'I'm aware of the terms of his incarceration,' snapped Judge Billings. 'Now, let him out.'

Billings watched Gunderson saunter off upstairs to let Zeb out and then turned to saloon owner, Bob Wessels. 'Now I've ordered they pay restitution of one hundred dollars to you for the incident. Does that seem reasonable to you sir?'

Wessels stammered, 'Ahh, well . . . '

'Good it's settled,' Judge Billings said hurriedly. 'Now I shall take my leave and return home. Good evening.'

'I'll walk you out, Judge,' said Jeb Coltrain.

Both men walked out onto the board walk and stopped just outside the lantern light that shone through the sheriff's office windows.

'Are you satisfied now? I did what you wanted,' the judge pleaded.

'Yes Judge, you did. Now when you get back home, you tell Shell to do what I said and your wife will be fine.'

Jeb watched Judge Billings hurriedly disappear down the darkened street. There was a noise behind the Rock Springs sheriff and he turned to see his brother emerge through the door.

'Come on, let's go.'

'Where we going?' asked Zeb.

'To find another saloon that we can drink at.'

'How on earth did you manage to get me out anyway?' Zeb asked curiously.

'Convinced the town judge to get you out,' Jeb answered.

'How?'

'It cost me a hundred bucks, but it cost the judge more,' he explained.

'Where's Shell?'

'He's takin' care of somethin' for me, now come on, I want a drink.'

While the two brothers found a place to drink, Shell Coltrain put out the lamps at Judge Billings' residence and locked the door behind himself.

14

The following morning, Laramie, Sally and Lonesome were ten miles from town, riding slowly along a rut riddled and winding trail, when the Mountain Pass posse appeared behind them. The galloping hooves that signalled the arrival of the posse, first sounded like the far-off thunder of a mountain storm, but as it got closer, Laramie could make out the huffing and snorting of hard ridden mounts.

Whoever was coming seemed to be in a hurry, so Laramie and the others pulled off the trail and waited for the riders to pass.

When they appeared around a blind corner, Sally was the first to recognise the rider out front who rode a Bay horse and wore a shiny star.

'It's Pa. Laramie it's him,' she called excitedly and eased her horse back onto the trail.

The posse eased down to a stop just short of where Sally sat, her horse side on across the trail. Her father was about to curse the rider who'd stopped them but had to bite it off when he recognised his daughter.

'Sally girl,' he said surprised. 'By golly it is you.'

Hank Richards jumped down from his horse and was met halfway by his daughter, he scooped her up in his arms and spun her around. 'It's so good to see you girl. I thought I'd lost you.'

'You probably would have if it wasn't for Laramie,' Sally conceded.

It was now that Richards became aware of the two other riders with his daughter. He stared at both before he said, 'I'll be damned, it is you.'

Laramie smiled. 'Howdy Hank, it's been a while.'

Hank Richards released his daughter and moved where Laramie could see him better. He had changed over the years, as had Laramie. Hank's hair was grey now and the years had transformed his face from young and tanned, to a hard-leathery look. He was strong and wiry and showed no sign of a stoop in his five foot eleven frame. He still carried a Colt .45, but in his saddle boot, instead of a rifle, Laramie noticed a sawed-off shotgun.

Laramie climbed down from Bo and walked across to his old friend. He stuck out his hand and Richards gripped it in a firm shake.

'It's good to see you Laramie,' he greeted. 'Is what Sally said true, did you help my girl out? Save her life?'

'I had some help,' the gunfighter said humbly.

Hank's eyes settled on Lonesome. 'How you doin' you old bandit?'

'I'll give you old bandit, just wait until I get down off this here cayuse,' the old mountain man grouched, 'I may be old but I'll still give you what for.'

'Calm down, you'll give yourself an affliction,' Richards smiled.

'I take it you two know each other then,' Sally guessed.

'Sure, we go way back.'

Richards turned his attention back to Laramie, 'How about you fill me in on the way to town.'

Laramie nodded and they all climbed back on their horses. The Mountain Pass Sheriff eased his horse up beside Laramie's. 'Well what happened?'

'Have you ever been to Rock Springs?' the gunfighter asked.

'Nope,' answered Richards as he shook his head. 'Never have.'

'Well don't.'

* * *

'And that's about all there is to tell,' explained Laramie.

Richards shook his head in amazement. 'That sure is one hell of a story. And Blackie Harbin's dead you say?'

'Buried him myself.'

'Can't say as he'll be missed,' Richards allowed. 'But there is one thing that worries me.'

'The deputy I shot?' guessed the gunfighter.

The Mountain Pass Sheriff nodded. 'Yeah, I'm goin' to have to look into it.'

Sally was shocked. 'Pa, you can't be serious!'

'I'm afraid I am, Sally,' he apologised. 'I'll get onto it when we get back to town, it's only another couple of miles. I hope you understand Laramie.'

'Are you goin' to lock me up Hank?' Laramie joked.

'I don't think I need to do that, do I?' Richards smiled.

'That's good. I need to get the old feller to see a doctor, have him checked out where he was shot,' the gunfighter explained.

'Don't worry, I'll take you there myself, he can check Sally out while he is lookin' Lonesome over.'

'I don't need no damn doctor,' the old man complained. 'I'm fine, them Blackfeet took good care of me.'

'He sounds fine,' said Richards with a grin on his face.

'I'd still like to find out how fine.'

Shell Coltrain rushed into the Gold Nugget Saloon and over to the table where his Father and Uncle sat with their shot glasses half full of whiskey.

'The Sheriff's back and guess who he's got with him?' he said excitedly.

'Davis?' asked Jeb Coltrain.

'Sure is. You was right, he's got the girl with him.'

'What are we waiting for?' asked the judge, new life coursed through him. 'Let's go get the murdering son of a bitch.'

The three Coltrains rushed out of the Gold Nugget and into the middle of main street just in time to stop the posse.

Jeb Coltrain raised his hand to stop them and spoke loud enough so that townsfolk in the general vicinity could hear clearly what he had to say. 'That's far enough Sheriff, we'll take Davis from here.'

The posse stopped and Hank Richards

studied the three men in front of him. 'And who might you be friend?'

'I'm Sheriff Jebediah Coltrain from Rock Springs,' he stated clearly. 'The feller on my right is my brother, Judge Zebulon Coltrain. This feller on my left is my deputy, Shell Coltrain.'

'You're a little off your patch aren't you Coltrain?' Richards pointed out.

'You might say that,' Jeb allowed. 'But these are exceptional circumstances. Your man there killed an officer of the law.'

'He tells it a different way, Coltrain,' Richards explained. 'Says it was self-defence.'

'He's a damned liar,' snapped the judge. 'It was murder.'

'He was tryin' to steal my horse judge,' Laramie spoke for the first time. 'When he didn't like me stoppin' him, he went for his gun. I had no choice. There were witnesses, they backed my story.'

'Well then, there should be no problem at your trial,' Jeb Coltrain observed. 'Ain't that so, Judge?'

'No damn problem at all,' he spat.

'That's not what my daughter says, either,' Richards added. 'And I'd believe her long before anyone else.'

'Your daughter is lucky I ain't inclined to prefer charges of aidin' and abettin' a wanted fugitive,' Jeb Coltrain said impatiently.

'You are a liar Coltrain, 'Sally cried. 'You left me with that animal Blackie Harbin.'

'Watch your mouth Missy,' the Rock Springs Sheriff said icily. 'I'd kill a man for callin' me that. As for that Blackie Harbin feller, he told me he was a friend of your Pa's. Guess he must have lied.'

'There is only one liar here Mister Coltrain, and that would be you,' Sally cried.

'He killed my brother,' Shell barked and his hand went for his gun.

Compared to some of the guns that Laramie had faced, Shell Coltrain was painfully slow. His gun had just cleared leather when the gunfighter's Remington boomed. The younger Coltrain cried out as the slug smashed into his gun and made it leap from his hand. Shell clutched at his arm as pain from the jarring blow radiated up it.

'Damn you, Davis,' he cursed the gunfighter through gritted teeth.

'Be thankful you didn't end up like your fool brother,' Laramie stated flatly.

'Sheriff are you goin' to stand for this?' snapped the judge. 'I demand you lock him up until we are ready to leave town. Then he will be transported to Rock Springs and stand trial for the murder of my son.'

'You know what Judge, I don't believe I will stand for it,' Richards conceded. 'So this is what I'm goin' to do. I'm goin' to take Laramie into custody . . . '

'No,' Sally gasped. 'You can't.'

Hank Richards turned to his daughter. 'Hush now girl, let me finish.'

He turned back to the Coltrains. 'Like I said, I will take him into custody and then I will do some investigatin' of my own to see what's what.'

'You got no right, Richards,' Jeb Coltrain said aggressively. 'The murder occurred in my town, so it's my case. Any investigatin' to be done, I'll do it, not you.'

Hank Richards knew the kind of justice Laramie would get from the Coltrains. 'I've said all I'm goin' to say Coltrain, now get off my street.'

'Just remember this Richards,' Jeb Coltrain seethed. 'You may have Davis now, but you have to be able to keep him.'

With that said, Jeb and the Judge started to walk off the street towards the Gold Nugget, Shell however bent down to pick up his six-gun.

'Leave it there kid,' Laramie said sternly. 'You won't get any more fool ideas if you ain't got it.'

Shell looked up at the gunfighter and saw that he still had his Remington in his fist, looked at his own gun, thought about it and then decided to follow the others inside.

'You can't be serious about lockin' Laramie up, Hank,' Lonesome said incredulously as he eased the hammer down on his Hawken. 'It's them varmints you need to be throwin' in jail.'

'I agree but it needs to be investigated,' he turned to Laramie who had holstered his gun after putting in a fresh load. 'I'm sorry Laramie, I hope you understand.'

'I understand Hank, you're only doin' your job,' the gunfighter allowed. 'Do you trust me enough to let me see to my horse and get Lonesome to a doc first?'

Richards nodded. 'Go ahead, I'll be waitin' for you at the Jail.'

Suddenly Lyle Gunderson appeared. 'Hey, Sheriff, did I hear some shootin'?'

Hank looked knowingly at his deputy. 'Have you been sleepin' again Lyle?'

Gunderson looked sheepishly at his boss. 'No, not really, but I do have somethin' to tell you.'

'Wait until we get over to the jail and

I'll listen to what you have to say,'
Richards said with a wink at Laramie.
'I'll see you in a while.'

★ ★ ★

'What did you say your name was
Mister?' asked the hostler curiously.

'Laramie Davis,' he answered.

'That's what I thought. You know
there are some fellers in town lookin'
for you?'

'Yeah, I met them earlier,' Laramie
said.

'Was that the shot I heard?'

'Maybe.'

The hostler's eyes lit up. 'Did you kill
one of 'em?'

'Blood thirsty critter ain't he,' Lonesome commented.

'No, I didn't kill one of them,' said a
frustrated Laramie. 'Now, can you take
the horses or not?'

'Sure, I can!' the hostler exclaimed.
'No need to get narky about it.'

Once the horses were settled, the two

230

men found the doctor's office and Laramie left Lonesome to get checked out then he went on over to the jail.

There he found both Hank and his daughter waiting for him, in heated discussion.

'Surely that must tell you something Pa, at least what type of people you are dealing with?' Sally said stubbornly.

Hank Richards rolled his eyes. 'For the last time, it's my job. I'll look into the other matter while I'm out.'

Laramie smiled at the pair. 'If you want, I can come back.'

The Mountain Pass Sheriff looked at him in exasperation. 'She's just as stubborn as what her mother was. You were a Marshal, you explain it to her.'

Laramie shook his head. 'Nope, I try to make a point of stayin' out of family squabbles.'

Richards' face took on a more serious expression. 'Speakin' of families, it seems there was some trouble with the Coltrains while I was gone.'

'How's that?' Laramie asked curiously.

'The Judge feller beat up on one of Bob Wessels' girls from The Royal Flush and damned near killed her.'

Laramie frowned. 'Why isn't he in jail for it?'

'That's the strange part,' Richards added. 'He was. Lyle locked him up.'

'So, what happened?'

'The brother, Jeb, turned up here with Judge Billings who ordered him released upon payment of a hundred-dollar restitution to Bob.'

'And that's strange?' asked the gunfighter.

Richards nodded. 'It is if you know Judge Billings. Normally he would have held a trial and given Coltrain thirty days.'

'Do you think his brother got to the Judge?' Laramie asked, but already knew the answer.

The Mountain Pass Sheriff exhaled loudly. 'Seems to be too much of a coincidence to me. Anyhow I'll go and see him after. I'm goin' to talk to him about havin' your trial here.'

'A trial!' Sally exclaimed. 'You can't be serious.'

'Sally,' her father said sternly. 'Go home.'

She set her jaw firmly and defied her father. 'I don't think so.'

'This is men's business young lady,' her father raised his voice a little. 'Now go home or I'll damn well put you in a cell instead.'

Sally Richards was shocked. 'You wouldn't dare.'

The Sheriff took a step toward his daughter.

She raised her hands in surrender. 'Alright I'm going.'

Laramie watched her leave. 'You sure do have your hands full there Hank.'

'Don't I know it,' he allowed. 'Now, where was I? Okay, I'm goin' to see Judge Billings about holdin' the trial here in town. I'll send word for the witnesses to come here as well as a Marshal.'

'The Coltrains ain't goin' to like that Hank,' Laramie said, stating the obvious.

'They will have their own problems,' Richards went on. 'That's what the Marshal is for. He'll be lookin' into them and Blackie Harbin.'

There was concern in Laramie's voice when he said, 'Be careful Hank, they might just slip a noose around your neck as well.'

'Let 'em try,' he smiled almost relishing the challenge. 'Now let's get you upstairs and squared away.'

'Are you really goin' to lock me up?' Laramie asked sceptically.

Richards smiled again. 'I'm goin' to close the door.'

⋆　⋆　⋆

'What in hell are we goin' to do now?' asked Shell Coltrain as he rubbed his arm where it still throbbed.

'Shut up kid, I'm thinkin',' Jeb snapped as he tossed down another shot of red eye.

'We can't let him do his own investigation Jeb, we'll never get justice

234

for Jeremiah if he does,' Zeb lamented.

The Rock Springs Sheriff remained silent.

'Well?' questioned his brother.

Suddenly Jeb had an idea. 'Send a wire to the Marshal's office, Judge. Apprise them of the situation. Say that the local Sheriff has overstepped his bounds and that he's harbouring a wanted fugitive. Get them to send word to hand Davis over to us. Go now.'

'And what if that don't work?' asked the Judge.

'Then we kill the Sheriff and take Davis anyway.'

15

'It says right there,' Zebulon Coltrain stabbed his finger at the piece of paper Hank Richards held. 'You are to release Laramie Davis into our custody and he is to be transported back to Rock Springs for trial.'

The answer to the Judge's wire had come back just after one in the afternoon.

'I can see what it says damn it,' snapped Richards. 'I can read, I'm not blind.'

'Well then,' the Judge smiled gleefully, 'go and get him. Bring him down here so we can leave.'

'No,' Richards answered flatly.

'What?' Zeb Coltrain couldn't believe what he'd heard. 'This here come from the Marshall's themselves. It says you are to give up your prisoner to us. What part of that don't you understand?'

Hank Richards turned his attention to Jeb Coltrain. 'If it is alright with you, I would like to get that verified.'

'No!' snapped the Judge. 'It's not alright.'

His brother was of a different opinion. 'That's fine Sheriff, you check on it all you want. But we'll be back before dark to get our man. Count on it.'

The Mountain Pass Sheriff stood quietly and watched the Coltrains leave his office before he took something from the old beat up cupboard against the wall and headed for the stairs.

Meanwhile, outside on the board walk, Zebulon Coltrain was beside himself, 'What in hell are you doing?' he hissed at Jeb. 'We could have walked out of there with him and had him hung before nightfall.'

Jeb shook his head and explained, 'No, he wouldn't have let him go without makin' sure it was all legitimate. This way he can check it out and see that it is all official.'

'I hope you know what you're doing,' the Judge said with a hint of menace in his voice. 'I mean to have him and if I have to kill that damn Sheriff to do it, I will.'

'If we can't get him Judge, I'll kill the Sheriff for you.'

* * *

Laramie heard the garbled voices downstairs in the Sheriff's office as he lay back, on the lumpy cot, in the corner of the cell. As much as he tried, he couldn't make out what was being said, but he guessed it would be about him.

He didn't have to wait long before he found out. Footsteps on the wooden stairs let him know that he was about to receive a visitor.

Hank Richards appeared outside the cell door with a grim expression on his face. Instantly Laramie knew it was not good news.

'You look like a man who just lost his

best horse. What is it now? Coltrain trouble?'

'Could it be any other at the moment?' he answered. 'They just turned up with a wire from the Marshal's office in Helena. It said for me to turn you over to them.'

'Ain't that somethin',' said Laramie in disbelief. 'Outlaws usin' the law for their benefit.'

'Yeah, it's somethin' alright,' Richards agreed. 'These fellers are startin' to irritate me some Laramie. But I told them I weren't goin' to hand you over until I checked out the wire first.'

'I bet they loved that.'

Richards snorted and said, 'They give me until sundown and then they're comin' to get you.'

'If it comes to that Hank, I ain't goin' down without a fight,' the gunfighter confirmed. 'Not to the likes of them.'

'That's what I thought you'd say,' the Sheriff said as he reached inside his coat and pulled out one of Laramie's Remingtons. 'Take this, just in case.'

Laramie swung his legs off the bunk and stood up. He walked across to the cell door and swung it open.

'Thanks,' he said as he took the weapon.

'If it comes down to it and the Coltrains come after you, the other one is in the cupboard downstairs,' Richards explained, 'and if they do for me, make sure my daughter is safe.'

Laramie nodded.

'I'll be steppin' out for a while,' Richards told Laramie. 'I need to track down the Judge. He wasn't in his office earlier so I will try his home. Then I need to check out that wire and see if there's been an answer from Rock Springs.'

'Watch your back, Hank,' Laramie warned.

'I always do.'

Laramie went back to the cot, put the Remington under the pillow and lay down. He preferred to meet his enemies head on and to be laid up in the Mountain Pass jail didn't sit well with the gunfighter. Even worse, he had to rely on Hank Richards to fight his battle for him.

He knew when it came down to it, there was only one thing that the Coltrains would understand. When they came for him, he would give them what they deserved.

★ ★ ★

Hank Richards' first stop was the telegraph office where the answer from his enquiries to Rock Springs waited for him. While he read it, Richards instructed Charlie, the telegraphist, to send the wire to the Marshal's office in Helena.

'How long until I get an answer Charlie?'

Charlie rubbed a hand through his thinning hair and thought for a moment. 'If you come back in a couple of hours I might have something for you then.'

Richards nodded his thanks and left

the office. He headed east along main street towards Judge Billings' house. It was easy to recognise the Judge's house, with the neatly trimmed gardens, courtesy of his wife who loved her flowers, and the white painted picket fence.

Hank swung the gate open and it gave a small squeak from a hinge that required grease. His boots crunched on the gravel path as he followed it to wooden steps that led to a timber porch. The front door was white and the sign on it read simply Judge Billings.

The Mountain Pass Sheriff knocked on the door and waited. After a couple of minutes, he knocked again, louder this time. Still no one came to the front door and Richards became concerned. The fact that the Judge could not be found at his office or at home was a worry. That the Judge had last been seen with Jeb Coltrain was most concerning of all.

Richards knocked one more time and

called out. Maybe they just couldn't hear him.

'Are you lookin' for the Judge, Sheriff?' asked a voice.

Hank turned around and saw that the speaker was the town's newspaper editor, Gray Lawson.

'Yeah as a matter of fact I am. Have you seen him about today?'

'Nope, I thought he might be unwell 'cause he never turned up for his regular chess game this morning.'

That did it, now he was convinced there was evil afoot, 'Gray, come up here.'

The editor came up onto the porch, 'How can I help?'

'Just stand there.'

Hank hit the door with all his strength and it burst open.

Instantly, the tell-tale smell of death wafted out the door, pushed by a cross draft from a partially open window.

'Oh my,' Lawson gasped as he held a hand up to his nose.

'Wait here,' the Sheriff ordered.

Richards stepped across the threshold and walked down a short hallway that opened out into the Billings' living room. That was where he found them both, laid out side by side with their throats cut.

'God, damn it,' Richards cursed out loud. 'Damn son of a bitch killed 'em both.'

He turned away from the macabre scene and walked back out onto the front porch where an ashen faced editor waited for him.

'Go and get the Doc, Gray, oh and the Undertaker too.'

Lawson asked hesitantly, 'Both?'

Richards nodded. 'Yeah, both. But keep it under your hat. I don't want it getting' around town just yet.'

'Fine,' he answered and hurried off to do what the Sheriff had asked.

Once the Doctor and the Undertaker had arrived, Richards went back to the jail. Lyle Gunderson had just finished his weekly clean of the guns in the gun cabinet. 'Get over to the Judge's place for me Lyle and keep an eye on things.'

'Sure, thing Sheriff, but what am I keepin' an eye on?'

'Someone killed the Judge and his wife,' he explained.

The shock was evident on the deputy's face. He went to speak but the Sheriff cut him off. 'Just go Lyle, now.'

So, without a word Gunderson left the jail.

* * *

Laramie cocked the Remington when he heard footsteps on approach. He levelled it towards the top of the stairs and waited for a head to come into view. When he realised it was Hank he eased the hammer down and slipped it back under the pillow.

Laramie could tell something was wrong, something bad. 'What's up?'

'The Judge and his wife are dead,' he said angrily. 'Somebody cut their throats and there'll be no prizes for guessing who.'

Laramie understood what he meant. 'Coltrains.'

'It had to be,' Richards confirmed. 'Jeb Coltrain was the last man he was seen with. Before I left the Judge's house the Doc told me they'd been killed last night.'

'Give me a badge Hank and we'll go round 'em up,' said Laramie as he tucked the Remington into his belt.

The Sheriff shook his head. 'I can't. You are still meant to be under arrest for killin' a peace officer. And before you say it, I know it was self-defence and I'm certain they killed the Judge, but I need proof. The wire came back from Rock Springs and from the looks of it you'll be in the clear, although I'm still waitin' on the one from Helena.'

'So, what are you goin' to do?'

'I'm goin' to check at the telegraph office to see if that wire has come through yet and I'm goin' to ask around to see if anyone saw anythin' last night.'

There was a rush of footfalls on the stairs and before both men knew it,

Sally appeared at the top of the stairs.

'Is it true?' she asked. 'Did someone murder the Judge and his wife?'

'Yes, it's true,' Hank confirmed the news to his daughter.

She gasped with shock and placed a hand to her breast. 'How terrible, who would do such a thing?'

'We have an idea,' answered Laramie.

'Who?' she asked before it dawned on her. 'The Coltrains?'

'We suspect it was them,' her father allowed.

'What are you going to do?'

'I'm goin' to ask around to see if anybody saw somethin' that might help. As of this moment I don't have proof. And you are goin' to stay here.'

'But Pa . . . ' Sally started.

'No buts, you're stayin' and that's final. Laramie keep an eye on her.'

Before Sally could say any more, her father was gone, down the stairs.

* * *

'Has an answer come back from Helena yet Charlie?' Richards asked the telegraphist.

The man smiled. 'Got it right here Sheriff, hot off the wire.'

Richards took the piece of paper and read it. He then folded it and tucked it into his jacket pocket.

'Charlie, I need you to send me one more wire and wait for an answer,' the Sheriff said as he picked up the stub of a pencil and a small sheet of paper.

Richards wrote out what he wanted sent then gave Charlie the piece of paper. The telegraphist read it and looked questioningly at the Sheriff.'

'The Judge and his wife are dead?' he asked with raised eyebrows.

'Afraid so Charlie,' he said and left the stunned telegraphist to send the wire.

* * *

The Gold Nugget was half empty when Richards entered through the bat-wing doors. He figured that was the effect the Coltrains had on people.

He sidled up to the bar and ordered a beer. Mose, the Negro barkeep was working the afternoon rush, except it wasn't a rush at all.

The barkeep gave Hank his beer and he took a large mouthful before putting it down on the scarred counter top.

'Kinda quiet in here this afternoon Mose, is one of the other saloons in town givin' away free booze?'

Mose picked up a shot glass and cleaned some dust off it. 'No sir, it's them Coltrains. Nobody wants to be around 'em since that incident at The Royal Flush. And now with the Judge and his wife turnin' up dead, well let's just say you don't have to look no further than right here.'

Hank's interest suddenly piqued. 'Have you heard somethin' Mose?'

'I was talkin' to a customer a little while ago,' Mose explained, as he kept an eye on the Coltrains. 'He told me that he saw that young feller down by the judge's last night.'

'Is he sure it was him?'

'Yes sir, he seemed mighty sure of what he seen,' Mose affirmed.

'Who was it Mose?'

The barkeep backed off a little. 'Well, I'm not sure if I should say Sheriff. This feller was awful scared. He only told me cause he needed to tell someone.'

Hank's voice hardened. 'Tell me Mose. Tell me who it was now.'

Mose dropped his gaze. 'It was Will Humphries.'

★ ★ ★

The bell above the door jingled as Hank Richards entered the General store. Will Humphries had just finished serving a customer so the Sheriff held the door ajar for them.

'Thank you, Adeline, be seeing you next week.'

'Goodbye Mister Humphries,' on her way out the door. 'Thank you Sheriff.'

Richards touched his hat brim. 'Ma'am.'

After the lady had left, Richards closed the door, locked it, turned the sign in the window and pulled the blind.

'This looks awful serious Sheriff,' Humphries said warily, then in jest, 'You don't plan on robbing the place, do you?'

'I want to have a chat to you about what you saw last night, Will,' Richards elaborated.

The store keeper's face gave into the distress that rested just below the surface of his false exterior. 'Oh, God. I knew I shouldn't have told that damn Mose anything. I just should've kept my mouth shut. Now they'll kill me too.'

'Now just calm down Will, they ain't goin' to be killin' anybody else. Now, Mose said you saw that young feller last night.'

Humphries nodded. 'Yes I did.'

'Would you care to elaborate Will?' Richards urged.

'It was late and I remembered I'd forgotten to lock the back door of the store. So, I came out and checked it.

Sure, enough it was still unlocked,' he paused for a moment and continued, 'Then I was just about home when I saw Judge Billings' door open. I was about to call out to him when I saw the young Coltrain feller come out.'

'Did he see you?' Richards asked.

'No, I don't think so. I guess if he did, I would have received a visit from them by now. Under the circumstances and all.'

'Why didn't you tell Gunderson, or even me after you'd heard what happened?' the Sheriff asked tersely.

'I'm scared Sheriff,' Humphries answered honestly.

'Are you prepared to testify in court to what you saw?' Richards asked.

'Do I have to?' Humphries asked stupidly.

'Of course, you damn well have to, he killed two people,' snapped the Sheriff. 'Did you think you could just mind your own business and it would all go away. Damn Will, I thought you had more respect for the law than that.'

The storekeeper hung his head in shame. 'I'm sorry Hank, I can't.'

'Yes, you can, and you will,' Richards gave the storekeeper no choice. 'I'll arrest him and he'll go to trial. But I'll keep the witness' name secret until then. That way no one will know it was you until the time comes.'

Will Humphries nodded. 'Okay, it would seem I don't have a choice.'

'No,' Richards confirmed, 'you don't.'

16

'I don't like it Laramie,' Sally's voice was full of concern. 'He's just one man.'

'What about his deputy?' Laramie pointed out. 'He'll back Hank, won't he?'

'Yes, but I hate to say it,' she stopped and thought about whether to continue or not, 'he can look after a jail house, but as far as outlaws and such go, he just won't cut it. I've heard Pa say several times that he was concerned about how Lyle would behave when the chips are down.'

'Your Pa will be fine,' Laramie tried to give her a boost. 'I've seen him face down wild Indians with just a knife, and come out on top.'

Sally smiled at him. 'I think you stretched the truth a little there for my benefit.'

'Well,' he said smiling, 'maybe a little. But don't worry, I've seen your dad in some tight places before today and he's made out alright.'

'But he was a younger man then,' Sally pointed out.

Laramie smiled again. 'Weren't we all.'

Suddenly the sound of gunshots shattered the peaceful afternoon and Laramie was filled with dread. Something told him the Coltrains were involved and things were about to get much, much worse.

He'd had enough and decided that it was time to fight back. Laramie rushed to the stairs with his Remington in hand.

'Where are you going?' cried Sally.

Laramie stopped. 'It's time to settle it once and for all.'

He took the steps two at a time and when he hit the floor at the bottom, Laramie hurried to the cupboard where his other Remington hung in its holster. He buckled it around his waist and checked both pistols over.

The door to the jail burst open and Deputy Lyle Gunderson rushed through the door to come face to face with one of Laramie's cocked six-guns.

'Don't shoot!' he cried out, his hands shot straight up in surrender.

Laramie let down the hammer on the gun and put it back in its holster. The look of dread told Laramie that something bad had happened.

'What is it Lyle?' asked Laramie calmly.

'It's the Sheriff,' he blurted out. 'He was in the Gold Nugget. He's been shot.'

'Oh, good Lord, Pa,' Sally gasped, as she stepped from the stairs into the room.

'Who did it?' asked Laramie, as he looked from Sally to Gunderson, his anger started to bubble up.

'It was the Coltrains, they did it.'

'Is he still alive?'

'I think so. They were takin' him to the doc's.'

'Are you goin' to arrest 'em?' Laramie asked the scared deputy.

'I ... I ... I can't,' Gunderson stuttered. 'I'm not good enough.'

Laramie looked at him in disgust. 'You have that damn badge for a reason. If you can't do the job, take it off.'

Gunderson looked solemnly down at the badge, reached for it, then unhitched the pin and took it off. He crossed to the Sheriff's desk and placed the star on top of it.

The look he gave Laramie showed the pain in his eyes and Laramie almost felt sorry for him, but like he'd said, if a man can't live up to the job, he shouldn't be wearing the badge.

Gunderson turned away and walked out the door.

Laramie directed his attention to Sally. 'Go and find Lonesome, I think he's at the hotel, resting, I'm not sure. When you find him, tell him what is goin' on. If anythin' happens to me, he'll take care of you.'

'What are you going to do?' she asked, fear in her voice.

'I'm goin' to kill the Coltrains,' he said savagely.

* * *

When Hank Richards had left Will Humphries' store, he'd gone straight to the Gold Nugget Saloon. When he pushed through the bat-wing doors he stopped and looked around to see if the Coltrains were there. He'd found them sitting at a table drinking whiskey, in a corner off behind the Blackjack table.

Richards had walked up to the bar and signalled to Mose who was still working. The barkeep walked along the bar and stopped in front of the Sheriff.

'Give me a whiskey, Mose,' he'd said as he reached into his pocket for some money and tossed it onto the counter top.

The barkeep grabbed a half empty bottle from the shelf behind him and filled a shot glass for Richards.

'Did you find out what you wanted to know?' the barkeep inquired.

'Yeah, I did,' Hank tossed the drink back and turned the glass upside down on the bar. 'Do you still have that sawed off Greener tucked away under the bar?'

'Uh huh.'

'Go get it for me will you. And make sure it's loaded.'

Mose walked back along the bar to get the shotgun.

Richards turned and looked about the bar room. There weren't a lot of customers but he wanted to avoid shooting, just in case a patron took a stray bullet, hence the shotgun. He hoped it would make the Coltrains think twice about doing anything rash. If he could take Shell Coltrain in peaceably, then maybe the threat of a hang rope might make him a little more talkative.

He picked out a path he would take, a short, direct route to their table to cut down their reaction time.

'Sheriff?' Mose's voice was tentative.

Richards swung around and took the gun Mose held out to him. 'If this goes bad, keep your head down.'

The Mountain Pass Sheriff strode quickly between the tables toward the Coltrains. Some men scattered out of his way while others stood steady to watch what was about to happen.

Richards stopped in front of the table and cradled the shotgun in the crook of his arm.

Jeb Coltrain sat still trying to read the Sheriff's face. 'What can we do for you Sheriff? Are you here to tell us we can have Davis any time?'

'No, I came to tell you that we are goin' to hold a trial here in town,' the Sheriff smiled.

'You're what?' asked Zeb Coltrain in disbelief.

'You might find that a bit hard without a Judge,' Jeb pointed out.

'No, I sent for another one,' Hank explained. 'Should be here in a couple of days.'

'The hell you say,' a cold smile spread across Jeb Coltrain's face.

'I think you are forgetting that we have a wire informing you to hand Davis over to us,' reminded the Judge.

'I'm not talkin' about Davis,' he informed them. 'I'm talkin' about the young feller here, Shell.'

Jeb Coltrain's voice grew cold and deadly. 'Be careful with what you say next Richards. False accusations are liable to get a man killed.'

'Well now, let's see. I have a witness,' he told them, 'who saw the kid there comin' out of the Judge's house last night.'

'Lies,' said Zeb Coltrain vehemently. 'It's all lies. Shell has never been near that house.'

'My brother is right Richards,' Jeb agreed. 'He was with us all night.'

'I suppose I have your word on that?' he asked sceptically.

'You do,' the Judge said firmly.

'I think that I would believe the word of my witness over you three any day of the week,' Richards said, brushing aside their alibi for Shell, 'So this is what is goin' to happen. I'm goin' to arrest him on suspicion of murder. We are goin' to have a trial and let the jury decide if he did or did not murder Judge Billings and his wife. If I were a bettin' man, I think he'll stretch rope.'

Shell shot a glance at his father. 'Pa?'

'It's okay Shell, he's got nothing on you,' Zeb said to calm his son.

'Get up boy,' the Sheriff ordered. 'You're comin' with me.'

'No, he's not,' the Judge said defiantly as he rose to his feet.

Richards moved the shotgun and pointed it at the Judge. 'Don't do anythin' stupid Judge. This here scatter gun will make a fine mess of them clothes you're wearin'.'

Suddenly Hank Richards realised he'd made a mistake. He'd taken his eyes off Jeb Coltrain. He swung the scatter gun back to cover the Rock Springs Sheriff but was too late.

The table top exploded as the .45

calibre slug punched through it in a shower of wooden splinters and hit Richards in the chest. It knocked him back and in a reflex action, Richards' finger squeezed the triggers of the shotgun and it discharged its lethal load into the ceiling.

Jeb Coltrain lurched to his feet and tipped the table over as he went. He brought his cocked Colt up for another shot but it wasn't required. Hank Richards was down on the floor and remained unmoving.

The Rock Springs Sheriff moved his point of aim to cover the room but there was no threat from any of the men who just stood and stared at the still form of their peace officer.

Mose came out from behind the bar and hurried across to the fallen Richards. He knelt beside him to check his condition, all the time covered by the gun of Jeb Coltrain.

The bat-wing doors were thrust inwards and the doctor hurried into the bar room.

'You were quick doc,' a cow hand observed.

'I just happened to be passing by when I heard the shooting,' explained the medico.

The three Coltrains watched in silence as the doctor checked out Hank Richards, then he picked out four cow hands who stood watching the scene. 'Get him over to my office, before he dies.'

The doctor gave the Coltrains a disdainful look and followed the others out the doors.

It was out on the board walk that Deputy Gunderson ran into them and was filled in on the details. Instead of going into the saloon, he hurried forthwith to the jail.

17

When Laramie stepped off the board walk into the dusty main street of Mountain Pass, he did so with purpose. Long strides kicked up small puffs as he walked past the town's citizens who milled in the roadway and talked, in shock, about what had just happened to their Sheriff.

Then a man said loudly, 'Look, it's Laramie Davis. He's out of jail.'

'Oh lord,' said a woman worriedly. 'He's wearing his guns.'

Another man's voice spoke up, this one he recognised as the hostler. 'Now them Coltrains are in for it.'

People started to clear the street. They knew instinctively what came next. Men were about to die and they all secretly hoped it would be those murderers, the Coltrains.

Laramie was twenty yards short of the Gold Nugget when the doors swung open and the three Coltrains walked out onto the board walk. The gunfighter halted and stood rock steady, his eyes turned cold. The three men paused for a moment, spotted their quarry, then stepped down into the street. They fanned out and faced Laramie.

'Well, well,' sneered Jeb Coltrain. 'I guess you saved us the trouble of comin' to get you.'

Laramie said nothing.

'I see you have your guns too,' the Rock Springs Sheriff continued. 'Now what man in his right mind would let a wanted murderer like you have his guns back?'

Still Laramie said nothing.

'I guess brother Jeb, that he will just have to be shot, trying to escape. I would have preferred hanging but, this will do.'

'Sorry about your friend Richards,' Jeb's apology dripped with sarcasm. 'But he had some fool idea that Shell here killed the town Judge. It took a little convincin' but he saw the error of his ways in the end.'

Jeb Coltrain smiled wickedly. Laramie studied the situation. The Sheriff was his main threat so he had to be taken out first. The kid needed to be next. He couldn't see the overweight Judge being too much of a problem.

Laramie took a deep breath.

'Coltrain,' he said coolly. 'You talk too much, have at it.'

The smiling light in Jeb Coltrain's eyes extinguished and turned to a dark, sinister glint. All along main, the street was empty. Eyes peered out through small gaps in curtains, a macabre fascination with not wanting to miss the deadly action that was about to take place.

There was a moment when time stood still, a pregnant pause and then the four men went to work.

Jeb Coltrain's hand flashed down to his gun butt and his fingers wrapped around its walnut grips. In one fluid motion, his Colt was out and levelled at Laramie, but his finger never depressed the trigger.

Laramie's draw was still the fast, flowing motion that had made him legend throughout his time with the gun. Both Remingtons were out and dealing death in the blink of an eye.

Jeb Coltrain went down with a bullet to his throat. He dropped his unfired Colt and grabbed at the ghastly wound, blood flowed freely over his hands.

Shell Coltrain died on his feet when a slug burrowed into his chest, through his heart and ripped a gaping hole in his back.

That left the Judge. Surprisingly for a man of his stature, Zeb Coltrain was a lot quicker than he'd expected and had his Webley out and snapped a shot off in his direction before he knew it.

The slug tore into Laramie and he went down, the air knocked from his lungs and the Remingtons spilled from his grasp. Zebulon Coltrain cried aloud with glee, the lust for revenge blocked out the carnage that surrounded him. He walked slowly forward, gun pointed at Laramie, as he savoured the moment.

Laramie tried to move but his body was numb from the hammer blow of the Judge's bullet. If he could just reach one of his guns, but no matter how he tried, was unable to move.

The Judge stood over him, his eyes filled with tears of joy. He would finally get what he wanted. To be able to kill the man who'd murdered his son.

'How does it feel, killer?' the Judge asked happily. 'How does it feel to know you're about to die?'

Laramie could do nothing. He was helpless.

Thunder rolled once again down Main street and a third eye appeared in the centre of Judge Zebulon Coltrain's forehead. The heavy calibre ball from Lonesome's Hawken sprayed blood and brain tissue as it caused the back of the Judge's head to disintegrate upon its exit.

The Judge fell to the ground, the smile he wore became his death mask.

Lonesome's shadow fell across the wounded Laramie. 'Damn it son, I guess you're slowin' down in your old age.'

Laramie tried to smile but his wound hurt too much, so closed his eyes in grateful relief and passed out.

* * *

For two days, Laramie was laid up in a bed in the Doctor's residence. Across from him was a slowly recovering Hank Richards. His daughter Sally sat at his bedside and Lonesome sat in a chair by an open window. Both men were on complete bed rest for two weeks and at this point Laramie was ready to ride.

'Look at you two,' the old Mountain Man smiled. 'Not as young as you thought you were, are you? One of you gets hisself shot by bein' careless and the other needs an old man of my age to pull his chestnuts out of the fire.'

'Don't you ever stop old man?' Hank Richards mumbled.

'Sally,' said Laramie, drawing her attention, 'go get me my gun will you, so's I can shoot this damned old varmint and get myself some peace. Hell, I might even shoot myself just to make sure.'

'There we are,' the old man crowed. 'I save your life and not even a thank you. No sirree, you'd think that he'd be grateful, me bein' there for him and all.'

'Go away will you, head back to your cabin or somethin'. Just give us some peace,' pleaded Laramie.

Sally and Lonesome burst out laughing.

There was a knock on the door and the doctor entered. 'There's a young man out here wants to see you gentlemen.'

'Send him in Doc,' Richards said.

The doctor left the room and a couple of minutes later a tall man, wearing a United States Marshal's badge entered.

'Howdy Walt,' greeted Richards.

The man saw Sally sitting by her father and took off his hat. 'Hank, Miss Sally.'

'Hello Walt,' she greeted.

'Walt, this is Laramie Davis and Lonesome Lane,' Richards introduced them to the Marshal, 'this is Walt Jones. He usually stomps around this neck of the woods.'

They said their hellos and Hank asked, 'What can I do for you, Walt?'

'Head office wanted me to check out what was goin' on over here after the wires they received. So here I am,' he explained.

'Well sonny,' Lonesome offered, 'you're a bit late. Them fellers are long gone.'

The old mountain man elaborated on the events of the previous few days. He included what had happened after the gunfight with the Coltrains, and concluded with the burial of the three dead men.

'Sorry to waste your time,' apologised Laramie.

Walt smiled and looked at Sally. 'I wouldn't say that it's a wasted trip.'

Sally blushed, and asked, 'Would you care to come for some afternoon tea Walt?'

'Sure, Miss Sally, that would be great.'

Sally rose to her feet, and took the Marshal's arm. 'If you gentlemen will excuse us, we'll be going.'

'I'll talk to you later Walt,' said Hank. 'I'll fill you in then.'

The two of them left and Laramie said to Hank, 'I bet he jumped at the chance to come back over here.'

Richards shook his head. 'He's a bit slow that boy, I been waitin' for months for him to ask to marry that girl and it's like waitin' for spring thaw.'

'Have you give any more thought to what I asked you?' Richards enquired.

'I have,' Laramie answered, 'and I'm sorry Hank, I can't do it.'

'Do what?' asked Lonesome.

'I asked him to come on as my deputy,' Richards explained.

'And I said no,' Laramie reiterated.

'What are you goin' to do then?' Richards asked.

He winked at the Mountain Pass Sheriff. 'I know of an abandoned cabin in the mountains I might just use for a while to rest up.'

Richards nodded. 'You know what, I think I might join you.'

'What about the town? You don't have a deputy no more,' reminded Laramie.

'Walt can take over for a while, I'll clear it with the Marshal's down in Helena. I could do with some clear mountain air.'

Laramie watched as Lonesome got to his feet and walked towards the door. 'Where you goin' old timer?'

Lonesome turned and faced the pair, his steely gaze levelled at them, 'I'm goin' to get my trusty old Hawken, then I'm goin' home, and if I see either of you in my valley, I'm goin' to shoot you.'

Mumbling incoherently, Lonesome walked out the door. Laramie looked across at his friend.

'Do you think he means it?' Hank asked.

Laramie laughed out loud. 'I guess we'll find out.'

We do hope that you have enjoyed reading this large print book.

Did you know that all of our titles are available for purchase?

We publish a wide range of high quality large print books including:
Romances, Mysteries, Classics
General Fiction
Non Fiction and Westerns

Special interest titles available in large print are:
The Little Oxford Dictionary
Music Book, Song Book
Hymn Book, Service Book

Also available from us courtesy of Oxford University Press:
Young Readers' Dictionary
(large print edition)
Young Readers' Thesaurus
(large print edition)

For further information or a free brochure, please contact us at:
Ulverscroft Large Print Books Ltd.,
The Green, Bradgate Road, Anstey,
Leicester, LE7 7FU, England.
Tel: (00 44) **0116 236 4325**
Fax: (00 44) **0116 234 0205**

A TOWN CALLED INNOCENCE

Simon Webb

Falsely convicted of murder and sentenced to hang, it seems as though the end of young Will Bennett's life is in sight — but a strange circumstance of fate frees him to track down the real murderer. His journey takes him to a Texas town where he learns the truth about the plot that nearly sent him to the gallows. Bennett's journey from the town called Innocence to the final showdown with the man who framed him for murder ends in a bloody shootout, from which only one man will emerge alive.

INVITATION TO A FUNERAL

Jethro Kyle

At twenty-eight, Joseph Carver is the youngest college professor in the United States. He is estranged from his father Will, the sheriff of a Kansas town. When Will is gunned down during a bank robbery and Joseph's mother dies of grief shortly thereafter, he is forced to face his family demons and return home. After his parents' funeral, he arms himself and sets off in pursuit of the men who shot his father. His quest takes him into the Indian Nations, where he receives help of a most surprising nature . . .

MEXICAN MERCY MISSION

Richard Smith

After Sam's parents and sister are murdered by four bandits in a raid on their Texas homestead, the seventeen-year-old decides to ride south with his uncle, Marshal William Grant. Sam is determined to avenge the deaths of his family members. Across the Mexican border, they talk their way into a fortified hideout with the ambitious hope of rescuing a young girl who has been abducted by the same four killers. And on the way home, pursued relentlessly across the Rio Grande by bandits, they must face one final bloody battle . . .

COYOTE MOON

Ralph Hayes

Buffalo hunter O'Brien is settling down to a more civilized life in Fort Revenge, in Indian Territory, helping his friend run a stage line there. However, it isn't long before trouble comes from two directions: in the form of an outlaw gang from Tulsa who want to buy his friend's stagecoach company and won't take no for an answer, and from a family of killers who are seeking revenge for the death of their kin at his hands. O'Brien must respond to these challenges with his own brand of gunsmoke . . .